FINCH HOUSE

FINCH HOUSE

CIERA BURCH

MARGARET K. McELDERRY BOOKS

New York   London   Toronto   Sydney   New Delhi

MARGARET K. McELDERRY BOOKS
An imprint of Simon & Schuster Children's Publishing Division
1230 Avenue of the Americas, New York, New York 10020

MARGARET K. McELDERRY BOOKS is a trademark of Simon & Schuster, Inc.
For information about special discounts for bulk purchases, please contact Simon & Schuster Special Sales at 1-866-506-1949 or business@simonandschuster.com.
The Simon & Schuster Speakers Bureau can bring authors to your live event. For more information or to book an event, contact the Simon & Schuster Speakers Bureau at 1-866-248-3049 or visit our website at www.simonspeakers.com.
Interior design by Steve Scott
The text for this book was set in Bitstream Cooper Light.
Manufactured in the United States of America
0722 FFG
First Edition
2 4 6 8 10 9 7 5 3 1

Library of Congress Cataloging-in-Publication Data
Names: Burch, Ciera, author.
Title: Finch house / Ciera Burch.
Description: First edition. | New York : Margaret K. McElderry Books, 2023. | Audience: Ages 8–12. | Audience: Grades 4–6. | Summary: When eleven-year-old Micah's grandfather goes missing, her instincts lead her to the off-limits Finch House, but when a boy named Theo invites her in, Micah realizes she cannot leave and must convince the house to let her go.
Identifiers: LCCN 2023006369 (print) | LCCN 2023006370 (ebook) | ISBN 9781665930543 (hardcover) | ISBN 9781665930567 (ebook)
Subjects: CYAC: Haunted houses—Fiction. | Friendship—Fiction. | Grandparent and child—Fiction. | Grandfathers—Fiction. | African Americans—Fiction. | LCGFT: Paranormal fiction. | Novels.
Classification: LCC PZ7.1.B8725 Fi 2023 (print) | LCC PZ7.1.B8725 (ebook) | DDC [Fic]—dc23
LC record available at https://lccn.loc.gov/2023006369
LC ebook record available at https://lccn.loc.gov/2023006370

For the best poppop a girl could ask for.
I would definitely brave a haunted house
to find you, Pop.

FINCH HOUSE

chapter one

Micah was, she reassured herself, faster than a garbage truck. She had to be, or she'd woken up early for nothing. Besides, she wanted that bookshelf. Sitting on the curb in front of a small white house, it was the most colorful thing on the snow-covered street—bright purple with yellow and pink flowers painted down its side. It matched the new bedspread her mom had bought her perfectly, which meant it would look great in her new room.

If she managed to outrun the garbage truck.

"Wait!" she yelled as it came to a stop.

The garbage woman, dressed in a bright yellow vest, making her the second most colorful thing on the street, frowned at Micah as she stopped too. It took all her balance to keep from toppling over into the nearest snow pile as she leaned over to catch her breath.

1

"Sorry." She panted. "One sec. I just need . . ." She gestured into the air as if what she needed—breath, energy, more sleep—could be found in it.

"I don't have all day, girl," the garbage woman said. She looked more confused than annoyed, but Micah didn't want to give her time to cross that line. She straightened up quickly, readjusting her coat.

"Right! So, um."

She bit her lip. She didn't know how to say "Don't take the trash even though that's your job because I want it." This wasn't usually how networking went for her and Poppop. Usually, they were up early enough to beat the garbage trucks, or they came the night before garbage day, when all the things on the curb were newly banished from whatever houses they'd been in.

But she'd begged him to bring her out this morning. Anything to avoid packing up the rest of her room. Anything to spend a little more time with him. She'd spent most of the eleven years she'd been alive living at his house: going networking, or "digging through other people's trash," as her mom liked to tease, on weekends and riding shotgun in his pickup truck after school.

And now she was moving a whole hour away.

But she couldn't tell the garbage woman all that. Not when she looked ready to toss her in the back of the truck along with everything else.

Instead, she blurted out, "I like trash."

The garbage woman nodded slowly. "So, do you want future career advice, or . . . ?"

"No! I mean, no, thank you." She pointed to the bookshelf. "I just want that particular bit of trash. For my room. Please."

Laughing, the garbage woman walked around and hefted the bookshelf onto her shoulder. Micah's heart sank. She'd run all the way down the street and made a fool of herself in front of a stranger for absolutely no—

"I gotta get back to work," she said, "so tell me where you want this thing to go."

Once the bookshelf was successfully in the bed of the truck and the garbage woman was back in her own, Micah leaned her seat as far back as it would go and squeezed her eyes shut. She waited for the truck to rumble to life beneath her. She peeked an eye open when it didn't to find Poppop smiling down at her.

"It's gonna get pretty cold if we just sit here, you know."

He chuckled. "Didn't think you'd mind, what with how eager you were to leave the house this mornin'. Up before the sun, even."

She yawned at the reminder, and his smile widened. Out of anyone's smile, Micah was pretty sure Poppop's was her favorite. She liked the way it made his eyes crinkle at the edges and how his one gold tooth always seemed to catch the light.

Today, though. Today it made her sad. In just a week she'd only get to see that smile through the phone or after an hour in the car. She couldn't even ride her bike back to see him because it was so far. She wouldn't be able to tease him every morning about his growing bald patch or nag him to wear his reading glasses or remind him to take his meds. If she and her mom were gone, who would do those things?

Micah blinked back tears. Her hand drifted automatically to her wrist, twisting the silver bracelet that had belonged to Nana until she felt the heart-shaped charm rub against her skin. She hadn't eaten breakfast, and her stomach ached with the reminder.

"Turtle."

Poppop's voice was soft. The kind of soft that meant they were going to talk about things, probably her feelings. But she didn't want to talk. Not about the move, anyway.

"Do you think breakfast water ice is a thing? Because if Tina's is open, we should go there next. I think they have that weird hot chocolate flavor I've been wanting to try and—"

"Phones exist, Turtle."

"What?"

"Phones." He beeped the horn softly. "And cars. And your room at the house is always yours."

He reached over to pull her seat up until they were sitting face-to-face. "It's just time for you and your mom to have your own space now, is all. Change makes growth."

She frowned. "Maybe I don't wanna grow."

He laughed. "It happens whether or not you want it to, Turtle. Embracing it usually makes it a little easier."

When she kept quiet, he took her hand. "What's the worst you think will happen if you move?"

"I won't see you. Or spend time with you. And without us or Nana, you'll be . . ." Tears filled her eyes faster than she could blink them back. She looked down at their clasped hands. "You'll be alone."

Poppop squeezed her hand. "Just more change. More

growth. Besides." He smiled. "Just gives me a reason to visit my favorite granddaughter often."

She couldn't help but laugh. "I'm your only granddaughter."

"Exactly why you're my favorite. Now, how about we go get some hot chocolate water ice and leave our worries for a later day?"

Micah grinned. "Okay," she agreed. "But then I wanna see if I can catch up to any more garbage trucks. If I keep practicing, I think I can get pretty good at it."

chapter two

Moving was not fun.

Her mom was a tornado of energy, walking from one end of the house to the other and throwing everything she saw into boxes or asking Micah why she wasn't packing. And the answer was that every time she packed something away, she realized she needed it an hour later.

Her shoes? Nope, that one pair of winter boots was her favorite.

Her summer clothes? What if her mom surprised her with a trip to Hawaii and she had no clothes to bring? No way.

Her toys? She didn't know what she'd be in the mood to play with between then and the move, and sorting through them just made her want to play with them all. She couldn't do it.

She thought goodbyes with her friends and classmates might be hard, but instead, they just didn't exist. Winter break meant almost everyone was out of town. It was why Micah found herself alone the next morning, bicycling through the neighborhoods bordering hers. She tried to pedal fast enough to keep the cold away, but it crept in through the gap in her scarf and the spaces between her buttons.

Still, she didn't want to go home. Not when it didn't feel like home. With her mom and Poppop both at work, all there was were boxes and a whole life to pack in them.

So, she biked.

She didn't even realize she was following her favorite route until familiar places started flying by. The car wash Poppop called overpriced. The grocery store. The bank. Her old elementary school, with the playground that looked small to her now. There were a few little kids and their parents taking advantage of winter break there, buttoned up so tightly in their coats that they looked like giant marshmallows running around.

It wasn't until she turned a corner onto Tipton Street, lined with towering, leafless oak trees, that she realized she was heading for one house in particular: Finch House.

All the houses on Tipton Street were the kind Pop-pop called "richy rich." Most of them were huge, with gigantic green-even-in-winter lawns and backyards with pools. Some of them had multiple cars in the driveway. One even had a circular driveway with a fountain in the middle of it.

But none of them even came close to Finch House.

A towering yellow Victorian, it was the second to last on the street, with trim like lace curving along the roof, a half dozen thin, rectangular windows covering almost every inch of the front, and—Micah's favorite part—a huge Rapunzel-like tower jutting up into the sky.

It looked like a doll house. Or, it would have, if anyone ever bothered to clean it up. What was supposed to be bright yellow was closer to grayish cream. The front porch was missing boards, and the roof sagged. Even the grass, when it wasn't covered in snow, was brown and overgrown with weeds year-round.

Micah loved it. It was beautiful and creepy and looked like it had a story to tell.

The problem was: she wasn't supposed to go near it.

Poppop had said so the first time she'd ever seen Finch House, after he'd made a wrong turn on their usual networking route. She'd barely had time to look at the house before they were turning back around in the cul-de-sac and driving away from it, faster than he usually drove.

"I don't want you coming down this street, Micah," he'd said, glancing at her in the mirror. She'd still sat in the back seat then, and she'd nearly twisted herself into a pretzel trying to stare out the back window at it. "Or to that house. Nothing good's down here. Can you promise me?"

She didn't know anything about the house or the street. She'd never even seen it before. So she didn't see how a promise could hurt, especially when Poppop looked so serious.

"Sure," she'd said easily, turning fully back around. "I promise."

She ignored the guilty fluttering in her stomach now as she slowed down. The wind blew dark curls into her mouth and across her eyes, which widened in anticipation.

And there it was.

Finch House.

Only it was wrong. The roof no longer sagged, and the lights were on in its many windows. The walkway leading up to the restored porch was shoveled. There was even trash set out on the curb. Micah fumbled to brake before she could tumble off her bike in shock. For a moment, all she could do was stare.

It had only been a few weeks since she'd last snuck off to visit. But that was long enough for someone to clean up Finch House, apparently.

And to move in.

Sure, her mom always said change happened as quickly as time moved, but she'd never seen it happen so fast. She hadn't even seen a For Sale sign.

She was getting really tired of change.

Micah bit back a scream when a pile of snow moved. Before she could run, or even think to, a red-cheeked, dark-haired boy popped up and grinned at her.

"Hi," he said, like popping up from snow piles was something he did every day. A small brown and white dog popped up next to him. Micah took a step back as it shook snow off its fur, trying to get her racing heart under control.

"Is lying in the snow a habit of yours?"

The boy stood, brushing snow off his pants. He shrugged. "It's better than being inside. I'm Theo."

"Micah." She looked past him. "Do you live in Finch House?"

"I didn't know it had a name, but yeah." He stuffed his hands in his pockets, and Micah zipped her jacket higher. Just looking at him made her cold. "We moved in a couple days ago."

"What did you *do* to it?"

Theo frowned, craning his head back to look at the place. "Dunno. It looked like this when I got here. Was it different before?"

She nodded. It wasn't a completely different house. It was just cleaned up. But it *felt* different. The mystery of wondering who'd lived there, who'd left it, was gone now that people had moved in. So was how unique it felt nestled between two big, boring houses. She wondered if being all cleaned up, with people living inside, was weird for the house. Not that she thought the house could feel things like, well, weirdness, but maybe it didn't like it as much as she didn't like the thought of moving.

"So," Theo said, "do you live around here?"

Micah shook her head absently. Her eyes didn't leave Finch House.

"Micah?"

She blinked. "Sorry. What?"

"I asked if you live around here."

"Oh. No, I don't. I was just riding my bike around, mostly. I come to look at Finch House sometimes because it's cool, and no one's lived here in forever. But there's never any—oh!" She turned away from the house and Theo to look at the curb. For once, it was covered in stuff. Boxes and furniture, even a broken desk half-buried in snow. She took it all in, brimming with excitement, before rushing over.

"You're getting rid of all this?" she asked Theo over her shoulder.

He walked over to join her. "Most of it was here already. Inside, I mean. The last people that lived here left quickly or something, back in the eighties."

"Really?" Micah knelt next to an old wooden chest. It was about the size of a toy box, covered in flaking white and blue paint and shut tight with a golden latch. "Why'd they leave?"

"I don't know."

"This place has been around since my poppop was little," she said. "He probably knows."

She didn't really know what he knew. He hadn't talked about Finch House since he'd told her to stay away from it, not even when she asked. But she remembered his face the day he'd made her promise not to come back here. It had been so serious, so unlike him. She had a feeling he knew a lot about Theo's house. Way more than he'd tell her.

"Did he used to live here too?" Theo asked. He spun the top of an old, faded globe and stopped it with his finger. It landed somewhere in the Pacific Ocean.

She shook her head. "He couldn't. I'm pretty sure that was illegal when he was little. Segregation, you know? Certain people were only allowed to live in certain places?"

Theo's cheeks burned red. "Right," he mumbled. "Sorry."

Toying with the chest's golden clasp, Micah decided to save him from his embarrassment. "Hey," she said, "do you know what's in here?"

His face lit up with recognition. "It used to be my sister's. There are a bunch of old movies in there—VHS or something? Like, really old DVDs, basically."

Micah smiled. She knew what VHS tapes were. Some of Nana's favorite movies had been on them. They'd watched *Titanic* at least once every visit, the movie so long that it took up two whole tapes. She'd thought the grainy quality was weird, but Nana had loved it. She'd said that movies, even watched at home, should have a movie theater feel to them, like they were being pro-jected right onto the TV. She'd had a box for all her tapes, which she kept in the closet in the den. It wasn't as pretty as the one that had belonged to Theo's sister, but Micah had loved watching Nana pull it out to choose a movie.

It was buried deep in the hall closet now, with the rest of Nana's stuff no one dared to touch. She doubted her mom would let her bring it to their new house.

"Do you care if I take this?" she asked.

Theo shrugged. It seemed like a habit of his. "Sure, it's all yours. But, uh"—he glanced over at her bike—"how are you going to carry it?"

In her excitement, Micah had forgotten that Finch House was off-limits. Sometimes on her bike rides, when she found a new neighborhood or something that she thought Poppop would love, she'd call him. He'd always show up as fast as he could, just as excited as she was to see what she'd found.

But it wasn't excitement on his face as he parked and

stared at the yellow house. It wasn't even surprise. No, he looked scared.

Terrified.

His face relaxed into normal when he saw her, but his eyes kept flickering toward the house. Up and down, from turret to porch, like he was waiting for it to grow a mouth and swallow him whole.

Micah waved, then gestured for him to roll down the window. He shook his head. When she pointed to the chest and acted out putting it in the back of the truck, he pointed to his watchless wrist.

"Michaela."

She blinked. Poppop never used her full name, not even when he was upset or she was in trouble. He'd cracked the window, just enough for her to hear him, and he spoke again before she could.

"I thought I asked you not to come here, didn't I?"

She couldn't lie. "Yes, but . . ."

He stared at her through the glass, waiting for an answer. All traces of fear were gone. Instead, he looked how he did when he watched football, all worried eyes and tense mouth. When she didn't add anything else, he asked, "Did you go inside?"

It was cold out, and it looked warm inside Finch House. She was pretty sure Theo would let her in if she asked, and she could climb all the way to the top of the tower to finally see the view from up there. But she'd been so focused on everything being thrown out of the house that she hadn't given much thought to exploring the inside.

She shook her head. The wrinkles around Poppop's mouth relaxed.

"Good." He glanced past her at the house and Theo. "Now say goodbye. We're leaving."

Micah turned to look at the house. Winter sunlight reflected off the windows. The turret jutted into the gray sky, eyes on every inch of the neighborhood from up there. Below it, Theo still knelt next to the chest, petting his dog and shooting her curious looks.

"But we're already here! Can't we just—"

"Michaela. Get in the car now, please."

She obeyed reluctantly, grabbing her bike to lift it into the bed of the truck. She muttered to Theo as she passed him, "I have to go."

"But what about . . . ?"

She shook her head. "I have to go," she repeated.

She slammed the door harder than she had to, but Pop-pop didn't scold her. He didn't say anything as he drove to the end of the street to loop around and head back the way he'd come. Micah turned to watch as the house and the chest and Theo started to fade away, going blurry in the smudged glass of the back windshield.

Theo lifted his hand in a wave. She lifted hers back.

Finch House watched them go.

chapter three

Micah sulked for the rest of the evening, and Poppop didn't say another word to her, not even during dinner. Her mom looked back and forth between them and tried to break the ice a few times before she gave up. As soon as the dishes were gathered and the table wiped clean, Poppop went up to his room. Her mom turned to her, eyebrows raised.

"All right, spill."

"Nothing to spill," Micah grumbled. She ran a yellow and green sponge absently over a plate. "Your dad's just being weird."

"'My dad,' huh? What happened? And don't say nothing. You're sulking, which means something happened."

When Micah stayed silent, her mom poked her side. Micah couldn't help but squirm away, her frown giving way to laughter as poking quickly turned into tickling.

"Stop!" She laughed, splashing her with soapy water. If her mom wasn't going to play fair, neither would she. "Stop, okay, I'll tell you!"

Mom crossed her arms with a satisfied smile. Micah dropped the plate back into the dishwater until it was hidden beneath a mountain of suds. "Well . . ." She drew out the word dramatically until her mom raised her eyebrows. "Finch House is all cleaned up."

She blinked. "Finch House? Really?" She gestured for Micah to get back to her chore and reached for the newly rinsed plate. She dried it carefully with a dish towel. "And how do you know that?"

"I *might* have ridden my bike down there."

"Might, huh?"

Micah nodded. Mom sighed. "He asked you not to go there."

"I know."

"You promised him you wouldn't."

"I know."

"And then you called him there."

It wasn't her smartest move. "I *know*."

Luckily, Mom let it go. "All right, so what happened?"

Micah explained about the lights and the trash and Theo and his dog. She talked about all the furniture and

20

boxes sitting on the curb like a gold pile. When she mentioned the chest, her good mood fell again. "That's when Poppop got weird. He wouldn't let us take it home. He didn't even get out of the car."

"He was probably just surprised, baby."

"I was surprised too, but I didn't get weird." At her mom's firm look, Micah sighed. "I just don't get it. He didn't explain. He never explains anything about Finch House."

That was, she thought, the worst part. Poppop always explained: where they were going or why he was using a certain tool or, once, how he'd gotten on the roof without a ladder. It was one of the things she loved about him. How easily his explanations came and how happy he seemed to give them. When her mom told her not to worry about something or used some version of "because I said so," Poppop always gave her a reason. Even if it was a silly one. Even if it didn't make sense. He *talked* to her. Treated her like she was a kid, maybe, but a kid worthy of at least some kind of answer.

But he hadn't said a word about Finch House.

"I think he's just processing, Micah. That house, people living there, it's a lot for him to deal with."

She frowned, scrubbing at a stubborn stain on a fork. Washing dishes was her least favorite chore, but every night her mom treated it like some sort of bonding ritual. "It's just a house," she grumbled. "A big, stupid, yellow house."

"And with houses come history."

"He never even lived there. Why should he care about its history?"

"No," her mom agreed. "But you don't have to live somewhere for it to be important to you."

Mom glanced at her. "He had a sister, you know. He never told me her name, but he did mention that she was older than him. A little older than you, too, when she went missing."

A glass slipped from Micah's hands and into the dishwater as she turned to stare at her mom. "What. Really?" She shivered, reaching for the glass, and turned on the hot water. The water in the basin was growing cold. "What's that got to do with Finch House, though?"

"The last time he saw her was there."

Micah waited for her mom to say anything else, biting the inside of her cheek as the seconds passed. Mom hated being interrupted. But she didn't say anything else, and Micah wasn't well known for her patience.

"Well?" The question burst from her on an exhale. "Where'd she go? Why were they there? What happened?"

Her mom finished drying the last of the dishes silently. She rocked up onto her tiptoes to place them in a cabinet before turning to Micah. "I don't know. It's all he's ever said about it, and it never seemed right to push."

Micah didn't understand. "Weren't you curious?"

Mom smiled and took her face in her hands. They were damp and slightly chilly, but soft as always. "Of course I was," she said. "But he was upset when he talked about it. And sometimes keeping people from hurting is more important than satisfying your curiosity. Right?"

Micah nodded, but she was skeptical. He would probably hurt whether he talked about it or not. But they wouldn't know the truth unless they asked. They'd just be curious forever.

When she didn't say anything else, Mom kissed her cheek. "If he wants to talk about it," she said, "he will. Otherwise, it's none of our business." She stepped back. "Your poppop'll come around. Just give him some time."

But what if he didn't? What if he never told them anything?

"Okay," she said reluctantly.

But she didn't need Poppop to find out everything about Finch House.

Before Mom went upstairs, Micah added, "Can I borrow your laptop?"

Google hated her.

So far, Micah had searched a dozen different things, including:

"Finch House"

"Missing girl Finch House"

"1950s missing girl Finch House"

"Finch House tipton street missing"

And so far, she had learned absolutely nothing. Her great-aunt didn't exist on the internet. And, for all that it was a novelty in their town, neither did Finch House.

At least, not by name. On page seven of too many millions of search results, a headline from a newspaper archive caught her eye.

TROUBLE ON TIPTON STREET? SIBLINGS, 7 AND 10, GO MISSING FROM BEDROOM OVERNIGHT.

The article, written in 1983, was barely a paragraph long. It didn't tell her much. Just the missing kids' names, Lisa and Ashley, and how they'd disappeared from their house, a yellow Victorian at the end of Tipton Street, on Monday night, just after they went to bed.

"No way," Micah whispered aloud. She glanced anxiously at her bedroom window before turning back to the laptop.

Still, an hour of searching later and she was back at a dead end. There was nothing about Poppop's sister and nothing about what happened to Lisa and Ashley. Once, she'd thought there was an article about another missing kid, but when she clicked it, the screen blurred and it wouldn't let her continue unless she paid for an account.

Her groan quickly became a yawn. She looked at the clock. It was one in the morning. The usual giddiness she felt at staying up past her bedtime bubbled up and was quickly pushed aside by a wave of sleepiness.

Clearly, the internet didn't know much about Finch House or missing girls.

She'd just have to ask Poppop in the morning and hope he didn't mention it to her mom.

Stifling another yawn, Micah shut the laptop and set it on the floor, then slid beneath the covers. Without the bright light of the screen, the glow-in-the-dark stickers on her ceiling were visible. A handful of constellations stared down at her. Lynx glowed the brightest. Cassiopeia looked like it could go out at any moment.

She shut her eyes, but sleep didn't come easy. All she could think about was Finch House. Why Poppop had been so insistent that she didn't go there. Why Theo's family had moved in. What had happened to her great-aunt and those sisters. There were more important things than satisfying her curiosity, Mom had said, but Micah thought she was wrong.

Maybe everyone else just hadn't been curious enough.

chapter four

Curiosity still fluttered like overeager butterflies in Micah's stomach the next morning. She woke up early, stumbling through the dark hall to Poppop's room. He always woke up early enough to say good morning to the sun, as he put it. Even in winter, when the sunlight was watery and weak and barely pierced the blinds.

She knocked on his door. When nothing happened, she knocked again, harder.

"Poppop?" she whispered. "It's me."

A small, annoying part of her brain whispered that he was mad at her. That it was her fault he'd shut himself up in his room the night before and that he didn't want to look at her, let alone talk to her.

She tried her best to ignore that voice. Taking a deep breath, she pushed open the door. She expected the room to be empty, thought maybe he was in the kitchen even though she couldn't smell coffee, but there he was. Sitting on the edge of his freshly made bed, staring at something in his hands. It looked like a picture, but she couldn't tell. She stepped closer for a better look, and the floor creaked, giving her away.

She winced. Poppop looked up. He slipped the picture into a small album, shutting it tight as he smiled up at her. "Up early today, huh, Turtle?"

She nodded, eyeing him carefully. He looked, well, normal. There was nothing worried or frightful in his expression. Nothing sad. If anything, he looked a little tired. But considering how early it was, so was she.

She decided to ask anyway. "Are you okay? 'Cause yesterday you seemed kinda . . ." She searched for another word and came up short. "Strange." She barreled on before she had a chance to stop herself. "Is it about your sister? Mom told me a little about what happened, but I wanted to know—"

He stood up abruptly. "I'm feeling peckish. What do you say about heading out to the bakery with me this morning?"

She blinked. Once a week, he went to Cornerstone Bakery as soon as it opened and brought home a dozen fresh doughnuts for Micah and her mom to wake up to. But today wasn't his usual day. "Sure, but—"

"It'll be a nice treat, what with you girls moving soon. Can't eat a dozen doughnuts alone, after all."

He moved quickly. The photo album went into a drawer. His Navy hat, usually on his dresser, was pulled down firmly on his head. His eyebrows rose as he turned back to her. "Well? We gonna keep chatting, or are we gonna get this show on the road? I don't know if you want to wear pajamas to the bakery, but—"

"Can we go to Finch House?"

Poppop froze. All his sudden energy and quick movements stopped. "No."

"I just want to go get the chest I left behind," she said quickly. "I won't go inside or anything."

"I told you I didn't want you going there. Plenty of other places to go if you feel like going networking."

"But you won't tell me *why*. If you just told me, then maybe—"

"I said no, Michaela."

Her hands bunched into fists at her sides. Already she could feel tears of frustration welling up. "Stop saying no. Tell me why. Please."

He shook his head. The sternness of his frown faded

until he only looked tired again. "She loved that house, but all it's ever been is trouble. It should've stayed run-down. And you should stay away from it, like you promised me." He took a deep breath. "So. Bakery, then who knows where. We haven't been on one of our drives in a while. We could make this a long one, find someplace new to go. Maybe a new beach like last time? It'll be nice and empty this time of year."

It sounded almost like an apology. Like an olive branch. But Micah didn't want an apology. She didn't want to go for a drive or eat doughnuts. She didn't want to sit on the sand and feel the winter chill off the ocean as she dug for shells. Today, all she wanted was answers. But Poppop didn't look like he was going to give them no matter what she said or did.

"I think," she said slowly, "I'm going to stay here."

He met her eyes, and she nearly changed her mind on the spot at the disappointment she saw in them. But he nodded. Her choice was locked in. There was no going back now. "I'll see you later, then, Turtle."

She tried ignoring her disappointment as he slipped past her, into the hall and downstairs. Even though it had been her choice, Micah felt a little abandoned.

She was nearly back to her room when she remembered the photo album and the picture tucked inside. She hesitated for only a second. Then it was in her hands, her heart pounding a thousand miles a second as she slipped quickly back into her room and shut the door.

She peeked out the window when she heard the truck start and watched Poppop pull out of the driveway without her. Then she turned her attention back to the album and opened the front cover.

When dinner rolled around, the photo album was still on Micah's mind. So far, she had narrowed her great-aunt down to two possible people in two separate pictures. In one, Poppop and an unsmiling girl leaned against a crooked fence staring straight at the camera. In the other, a girl's face was too blurry to make out. She'd turned toward the camera too quickly, everything about her half-blurry except for her dress and dark plaits. If Micah looked hard enough, she swore she saw a smile in the midst of the blur.

But Micah didn't have much time to spend studying the album. Not going with Poppop meant that her mom put her to work as soon as she realized she was awake. First, she'd cleaned out the storage bin from under her bed, tossing all the summer clothes that didn't fit her anymore in the donation bag her mom left outside her door. The same went for her shoes, her books, and even an old, embarrassing collection of stuffed animals at the top of her closet, which she took way too long going through.

In the end, the only stuffed animals she got rid of were a tiny white rabbit missing an eye and a purple bear she'd won from a fair a few years ago. The rest she stuffed into a bin marked for the new house.

Still, none of her packing took her mind off Poppop's sister. She had so many questions. What did she look like? What was her favorite color? Her favorite hobby? Did she and Poppop get along? Micah folded another pair of shorts and frowned into the box she placed them in. What, she wondered, had happened to her stuff after she disappeared?

There was so much to think about, to imagine, that Micah thought she might burst from the mystery of it all.

When Mom called her down to set the table, she already had a mental list of questions. Mom had said she couldn't ask Poppop about his sister, fine. But she could still ask about his childhood, couldn't she? Then he'd have to tell her *something*.

But her mom stopped her when she went to put down the third plate. "He's not back yet."

Curiosity soured in the pit of Micah's stomach. Guilt flooded through her instead. She'd upset Poppop two nights in a row now, enough this time that he didn't even want to have dinner with her. They were running out of time to spend together before she moved, and there she was, ruining it.

She poked at the broccoli on her plate and half listened to her mom talk about work, glancing at the door every few minutes. Poppop rarely actually came through the front—he parked in the back and came up from the basement instead—but she couldn't seem to shake the habit.

"No wonder you're not hungry," her mom said as she gathered up the dishes. "All your worry's eating you up instead. What's wrong?"

"Nothing."

Mom raised an eyebrow. "Not buying it. Want to try again?"

Micah sighed. Sometimes she wasn't sure if she loved or hated how much attention her mom paid to her. She wondered if it was an only-child thing.

"Just worried," she said.

To her surprise, her mom didn't question her further. She just kissed the top of her head and grabbed a nearby glass, piling it carefully on top of the rest of the dishes she carried. "Whatever it is, it'll work out. Most things do."

Most things. But not *everything.*

When Micah finally climbed into bed, after peeking out back (it was too dark to see if Poppop's truck was there or not) and knocking lightly on his bedroom door (no answer), worry was still a rock in her belly. It weighed her down, dragging her into a fitful sleep.

chapter five

Michaela Robinson woke up with a plan.

It kept her quick-moving and unafraid when she went looking for Poppop and couldn't find him anywhere, carrying her from toaster to kitchen table, out the door and on her bike before worry had a chance to catch up with her again. She'd follow her and Poppop's usual networking route and find him. She'd make sure he was okay, and then she'd ask him about his childhood.

It wouldn't be that hard. No different from biking around on a normal day. Besides, out of everyone in their house, he had the most predictable routine. On his days off, he ate breakfast and watched the news in the mornings, took walks and played chess at the park when it was warm out in the afternoons, then picked her up from school and helped her with homework . . . or found something more fun for them to do until they had to rush back home and pretend they'd been doing homework all along when her mom got there.

On the days he still worked, he was at his office.

But she already knew he wasn't home, and it was too cold out for chess in the park. And when she called the office, because it was too far away to bike, the secretary, Ms. Adicha, said he wasn't there.

Still, Micah rode by the park just in case. Then she biked to the bakery and the bank, past Tina's and the dry cleaners, and all the way up the hill to the diner Poppop loved.

She rode around neighborhood after neighborhood, pink-cheeked and numb-fingered.

Everywhere she biked past, slipped inside, or asked around, there was no Poppop.

Which left her with one place to check.

Finch House.

It wasn't just because she was curious, she told herself, or because she wanted to see it all cleaned up again. Besides home, it was technically the last place she'd seen him.

By the time she got to Finch House, though, she'd been biking for two hours and was nearly frozen solid.

Which made it even more surprising that Theo was there, lying in the snow and staring up at the clouds again. All but swallowed up by a puffy red jacket.

"Do you ever go inside?" she asked, putting down her kickstand and hopping off her bike.

He looked up at the sky instead of facing her. "It's haunted." When she kept quiet, he laughed and sat up. "I'm kidding. Kind of."

She decided to ignore the second part. "Why're you out here? It's freezing."

"Why are you?"

Micah frowned. "I'm looking for my poppop. Have you seen him?"

"The man you were with the other day?" She nodded, and to her relief, he nodded too. "Sure, I saw him yesterday afternoon. He picked up Renee's old chest, the one you liked. But I haven't seen him today."

Her heart leapt. Yesterday, Poppop had said no Finch House, and he'd looked serious. But he'd come to pick up the chest anyway. Why? Because she'd loved it? Because she'd been upset? Either way, it had been for her. She felt herself thawing from the inside out, feeling coming back into her fingers and toes.

"You're sure you didn't see him today?"

Theo shook his head. "No. But isn't that your truck over there?"

He pointed and Micah turned around. It *was* Poppop's truck. Dark blue and gleaming under the winter sun, it was covered in a new layer of frost. The frost made looking through the windows harder, but it was still easy to tell that the truck was Poppopless. She stood on her tiptoes to peer into the bed of the truck for more clues. She found none. Only the chest Theo had mentioned before, its soft-colored wood and carefully painted flowers dusted with snow.

Micah sighed. She'd found Poppop's truck. That meant he had to be somewhere nearby, didn't it? "Okay," she said. "Okay, okay. I need a plan. A new plan," she corrected herself. Her old one had gotten her this far.

She was quiet for a long time. Eventually, Theo asked, "Well, what's your plan?"

She groaned. "I don't know!"

Micah lowered herself to the grass. It was chilly and damp with huge patches of snow, and she grimaced as the snow seeped through her pants. She propped her chin in her hands and glared at the visible tufts of brown grass as if it were withholding answers.

Theo sat up and folded himself into a cross-legged position across from her. "We lived in an apartment before."

She looked at him. "What?"

He repeated himself. "It was okay. High up on the sixteenth floor. We had a balcony, but there weren't any parks close by. Not even playgrounds, really. Even at school, it was just a fenced-in basketball court. No grass or trees or swings. You could barely see the clouds because of all the skyscrapers." He shrugged, running a hand over the grass. "That's why I'm out here, even though it's cold. I like it. Nature."

"It's winter," Micah pointed out. "Everything's dead."

He pointed to a group of nearby pine trees. Brilliant green under a gray sky. "Not everything." She sighed, and he turned back to her. "Do you have a plan yet?"

"You were talking to me the whole time!"

"I thought it might make it easier if you weren't thinking so hard."

"Well," she said rather grumpily, "I've got nothing."

"Well," Theo said, smiling slightly. "I've got a bike. We can keep looking. His truck is here, so he couldn't have gone too far, right?"

Her stiff legs and frozen fingers wanted to protest. She was so cold she wasn't even sure she could stand back up. But she thought of Poppop and how he'd looked when he first pulled up to Finch House two days ago.

Then she thought of what Theo had said, how he'd come back here just for her, just for the chest.

"Okay," she agreed. "Let's go."

Michaela Robinson no longer had a plan. But she did have a friend, and that was, she figured, almost as good.

Micah and Theo rode up and down his street. And the next three streets. And half a neighborhood away. They rode for as far and as long as they could, and still. Poppop was nowhere to be found.

Micah slowed to a stop when they passed Silver Boot Playground yet again.

They were just going in circles now. They were no closer to finding Poppop than they'd been before they left Theo's house. They hadn't even found any new clues. What if there weren't any?

She frowned. She hadn't thought she could get any more worried, but there it was. Fluttering in her stomach. Tingling in her palms. Empty space in her chest where there should have been air.

"You okay?"

Micah startled, then sucked in a deep breath. "Fine," she said. She flashed her brightest smile. It faded quickly. "Just cold."

For once, Theo looked cold too. The tip of his nose and both ears were bright red, and he'd zipped his jacket all the way up to his chin. "We should go back to my house for hot chocolate. And, you know, to make a plan. We can't just keep riding around out here."

"Maybe *you* can't."

"We *both* can't," he said firmly. Still, a smile broke across his face, stretching across each wind-chilled cheek. "Besides, we have the best hot chocolate, I promise. Triple chocolate and peppermint."

A shiver rocked through Micah. Hot chocolate did sound nice. And there was the appeal of finally going inside Finch House too. Climbing the stairs to the top of the tower and peering down on the whole neighborhood. Basking in the sunlight pouring in from the huge windows.

But she'd made Poppop a promise. A promise that she'd already broken. Going inside might make things with him worse.

Still . . .

Micah ducked her head, blinking hard against tears and wind. What if something had happened to him? What if she never saw him again? She'd been so frustrated with him the last time they talked, and he had looked so disappointed.

41

A familiar sadness crawled its way up her spine and curled up like a kitten at the base of her skull. It made her head heavy. It was the same way she'd felt when Nana died. Then, she'd sat useless on the couch while Mom and Poppop called people and made arrangements and wiped their tears too quickly for her to be sure they'd cried at all. She couldn't sit still and do nothing now.

Not again.

Not when this was her fault.

Yes, she'd promised not to go in. But Finch House could be full of clues, if not about where Poppop was, then at least about what had happened to his sister. She could solve a mystery! And she could share it with Poppop when he came back home from wherever he was.

It'd be silly to give up that chance when Theo was inviting her in.

She'd just look around, see if anything looked old or like something she might have seen in the photo album.

If she didn't find anything, she'd go back home.

In and out, that was it.

Micah stood on the porch of Finch House and hesitated in front of the open door. She'd never gotten this far. She'd never even made it up the formerly overgrown path. But there was the door, pretty enough for a door. It was pale blue, and sitting atop the knocker was a golden bird ready to take flight. She glanced over her shoulder at Poppop's truck. The engine was off. Poppop wasn't sitting in the driver's seat watching her break her promise yet again. She turned back around with a sigh and, after touching the knocker lightly for luck, stepped across the threshold.

She held her breath and waited for something to happen.

Nothing did. There were no creepy shadows or whispering voices or—

She paused.

There *was* something. Just a moment of cold, different from the chill outside. This cold felt focused. Like fingertips on her cheek.

Micah whipped her head toward Theo. "Did you feel that?"

"Feel what?"

She frowned, eyeing him suspiciously. "Did you *do* that?"

"Do what?" he asked. He'd turned away from her, already in the process of taking his jacket off and hanging it on a hook by the door.

Reluctantly, she took her jacket off too. "I just . . . I thought I felt something."

Theo shrugged. He headed for the kitchen. "Maybe you did."

Ignoring the teasing in his voice, she followed after him. A thick rug softened her footsteps. Everything in the house was a deep, dark wood: the doorways, the floors, the stairs. All of it shone in the sunlight. And all of it looked old, like stuff she'd find in a great-great-grandparent's house. Not somewhere a kid her age lived.

Unlike in her own house, she didn't see any family pictures. The closest things were a few framed photos along the wall of the stairs, pretty images of places she'd never been. She wondered if Theo had.

She opened her mouth to ask and almost screamed as a brown-and-white blur came running toward her. It took a while to realize it was a dog, the same one she'd seen with Theo the first day they met. It sat at her feet, wagging its fluffy white tail and panting.

Micah didn't crouch to pet it. She eyed it carefully instead, barely noticing as Theo joined them until he kneeled beside the dog and scratched behind its ears.

"Micah, meet Paprika," he introduced them. "Don't

worry, she won't hurt you. She's the least scary thing in this house."

She didn't find that as reassuring as Theo seemed to. Still, she held out her hand for Paprika to sniff, giggling as her wet nose nuzzled her fingers. Theo stood and Micah followed him to the kitchen, Paprika's nails clicking on the floor close behind them. It was bigger than Poppop's by far, with an island in the middle as big as a dining room table and two separate ovens. It was hard to get a good look at everything, but she tried.

Despite how she'd felt at the door, it seemed normal. *Looked* normal. Micah was almost disappointed. She'd imagined creaky floorboards and hidden rooms and dust motes drifting aimlessly in empty rooms. She'd imagined the kind of silence that made your ears ring, that reminded you with every breath that you were alive. She imagined it being a lonely, hidden type of place to live. Like living inside a game of hide-and-seek—all the fun of hiding and all the fear of being found.

But, of course, that was when the house was empty and abandoned. A blank canvas for all kinds of daydreams.

Now it was just a house.

There was nothing scary about it, she decided. Not

unless you remembered that kids had gone missing there.

Had Theo's parents gotten rid of everything? she wondered. Would there be any clues about Poppop's sister left? Or had they all been put out on the curb with the chest?

"What's it like living here?" she asked.

"What, Theo didn't tell you about all the ghosts he's seen?"

Micah jumped. When she turned, a teenage girl grinned back at her. She looked like Theo, with longer, darker hair pulled into a messy bun, a sharp smile, and a nose ring.

Theo didn't bother turning toward her. "Shut up, Renee."

Renee didn't. She kept grinning as she looked Micah up and down, ignoring Paprika as she weaved between her legs. "You're sure you're not another one of his ghost friends?"

"I'm sure," Micah said. Wait. "Another one?"

"Ignore her," Theo said, placing a steaming mug in front of her. It smelled like peppermint. She wrapped her hands around it immediately, melting into the warmth as he took the seat beside hers, his back to his sister. "She's trying to scare you."

"Only a little." She ruffled his hair, laughing as he batted her hand away, then leaned down to pet their dog. "Is it working? I could go back upstairs and try to make my best horror movie noises. You know . . ." She paced back and forth a few feet away until the wood under her left foot gave a loud haunting groan.

Micah shivered. She couldn't help herself. She'd had so many daydreams, after all. "Are there really ghosts here?"

"No," said Renee.

"Yes," said Theo.

The siblings looked at each other. Renee laughed. "It's an old house," she admitted, "and Theo's always been scared of the dark."

He made a face at his sister. "Like you're not." He turned to Micah. "Everything creaks here all the time, just like that. And it gets really dark. Like, the darkest I've ever seen. Even if you leave the hall light on." He blushed a little, as if he'd admitted what Renee said was true. "It's like there are shadows everywhere, sucking up all the light, and things are always moving in them. *Kid-shaped* things."

Renee rolled her eyes. "Or you're just imagining it." She swiped his mug before he could grab it and took a sip. She made a face. "Ugh. That stuff's disgusting."

Theo snatched his mug back. "Good thing I didn't make it for you. Besides, I'm not imagining anything. Paprika doesn't like it here either."

"Do you guys know anything about this house?" Micah asked before they could start fighting in earnest. Theo looked annoyed enough to start one, and Renee seemed bored enough to indulge him. "Anything weird like . . . disappearances? Missing kids?"

She hoped they might have more information about Poppop's sister or Lisa and Ashley, the missing sisters she hadn't been able to find anything else about online.

Theo shook his head, but Renee perked up. She leaned forward on the island, her grin transforming into an eager smile. "Actually, yeah. Some kids I met were talking about how they couldn't believe we lived here. It's apparently a big deal in town or something? At least on Halloween."

She looked at Micah for confirmation, but Micah only shrugged. As far as she knew, it was only a big deal to Poppop. She'd never talked about it with anyone or heard anyone else talk about it until now. But she *did* know all about the pranks and dares the teenagers in town liked to play on Halloween. Once, she and her friend Diamond had only narrowly avoided being egged

48

while trick-or-treating. And every year at least one of Poppop's newspaper articles mentioned groups of teenagers sneaking into the cemetery or freaking families out by wandering around in their costumes in the middle of the night. Micah just hadn't known that Finch House was part of their weird fun.

"Anyway, a couple of years ago this freshman, Gavin, was dared to break in. All he had to do was see if he could climb to the top of the turret, then wave out the window to prove he'd made it. And he did, apparently. But." Renee lowered her voice to a whisper and leaned even farther across the island. Micah leaned in too, fascinated. "He barely had the chance to peek out the window before he was *yanked* back."

Renee threw herself back into her seat suddenly, too busy laughing at Micah's loud gasp to realize how close her chair was to toppling over. Her voice went back to normal after she caught her breath.

"That was it. The window slammed shut, and everyone waited for Gavin to come down."

Micah couldn't help herself, even as she spun her bracelet around and around on her wrist. "And?"

Renee shrugged. "And he never came back down. Some of the kids told their parents, and the police did a

49

little bit of searching, but everyone still thought it was a prank."

Micah frowned. The internet hadn't told her about that. She said as much, and Renee shrugged again. It was clearly a family habit. "I'm just telling you what they told me. They said it happens so often the cops and the newspapers just stopped writing about it. Instead, they put some Halloween curfew in place and called it a day."

Micah blinked. There *was* a curfew, but it was so far past her bedtime she'd never paid it any attention before. "Do you believe them?"

"That people could go missing here?" Renee shrugged. "Sure, it's huge. Do I think they got eaten by ghosts or something equally stupid? Doubt it."

"Then what do you think happened?" Theo challenged. He hadn't looked like he was paying the story any attention as his sister told it—he'd seemed more focused on watching Paprika settle into a black dog bed across the room—but his eyes were as wide as Micah's. "You can't just wander around a house forever. *Something* had to happen to them."

Renee rolled her eyes. "You two are so easy to scare, it's almost cute. That's all those kids were trying to do—mess with the new kid living in the haunted house and

50

see if she'd bite. I'd be friendless already if I bit as hard as you two did."

Micah felt embarrassment warming her cheeks even as fear still gripped her. Maybe that story had been made up, but her great-aunt *had* gone missing. Ashley and Lisa too. Who knew how many other people had?

She glanced around the kitchen and dining room. They were flooded with light, winter sunlight and warm orange overhead lights, but there was no rule that said that ghosts had to stick to the dark. They could be there at any moment. They could be there *now*, watching them, listening to them, even biding their time until—

"Dude, are you okay?" Renee's smile faded as she stared at Micah. "You look like you're about to pass out. I was only kidding, you know. Everything cool or marginally creepy about this place has probably been deep cleaned out of it. Ghosts included."

"Yeah," Theo said slowly, still frowning at his sister. "Mom and Dad said they gutted the place."

"They gut every place," Renee muttered. "Makes it nice and boring and easy to sell."

Shaking his head, he turned to Micah. "Let's go upstairs. Nothing will bother you."

He meant it as a kindness, but all Micah heard was that something was in the house that could bother her to begin with.

Still. She was here now, inside the house she'd spent forever daydreaming about, and her curiosity was just as strong as her unease. She was supposed to be looking for clues, after all.

That was probably why she paused at the bottom of the stairs to stare at a door set into the wall. It wasn't a proper door. It was only about half her height, and she nearly missed it at first since it was painted to blend into the wall. She crouched to look closer. Instead of a handle, there was a small keyhole, too small to even peek through. When she ran her hand along the wood paneling, there didn't seem to be any way to open it.

She looked up at Theo. "What's this?"

He crouched beside her. "Some kind of door. There are lots of them, almost one in each room, but none of them open. Well, almost none, I think."

"Almost?"

"There's one in the attic, but I haven't tried it yet." He bit the corner of his lip. "It's the weirdest one, right behind the door up there."

"Why is it weird?" Besides the obvious weirdness of a tiny door that didn't open.

"It just feels weird." Theo shifted uncomfortably. "Like the shadows, I dunno. I don't go in the attic that much. It's cold." He stood and brushed invisible dirt from his pants without looking at her. "Let's just go upstairs."

Micah frowned, looking at him even as he avoided looking at her. He wasn't telling her something, or maybe he couldn't explain it, but she was sure the problem with the attic was more than that it was *cold*.

Which, of course, made her curiouser. The maybe-ghosts and the shadows and the strange little doors, all of them scared her. But not quite as much as they fascinated her.

"Well?" Theo said, foot on the stairs, poised to head up. "Are you coming?"

She was in Finch House, and there were weird doors that didn't open.

She had to see it. She *had* to.

A warm flush of excitement went through her. Was that what her great-aunt had felt too? Some restless curiosity inside her that could only be soothed with answers that the house had? Did she find whatever she was looking for? Or had she kept chasing it until she got lost? Until she went missing.

Micah took a deep breath. She counted to five and waited for her curiosity to fade.

It didn't.

"I'm coming," she agreed. "But let's go all the way up. I want to see that door."

chapter six

There was nothing creepy about the attic in the middle of the day. Except for the fact that it was an attic. It didn't look like much more than storage space. Dark beams crisscrossed the ceiling, low enough in places that Micah had to duck, and pink puffs of what looked like foam were everywhere.

"It's supposed to keep it warm up here," Theo had explained, "but it doesn't really work."

Micah agreed. It wasn't just cold like Theo had said; it was freezing. As cold as if they were standing by the open front door. She'd nearly wanted to turn back around and grab her coat. But then he'd shown her the door. And she hadn't stopped looking at it since.

It wasn't much. Almost identical to the one downstairs except this one was completely smooth, lacking even a keyhole. Micah bent down and pressed along the seams of the door, hoping it would swing open like in the movies. She sighed when it didn't.

"Maybe it's not a door," she suggested. "Maybe it's just wires or something back there."

Theo nodded, but he looked unconvinced. He lingered by the door to the hallway like he was ready to flee at any moment. "I guess. But I . . ."

"But what?"

He sighed. "I've heard stuff coming from back there. My mom says it's just pipes, but it sounds like voices sometimes. Like how you can hear people talking through a wall."

The cold intensified. It tickled along the back of Micah's neck and down her spine. "Do you hear that only up here?"

"No." He met her gaze. He looked a little worried but mostly stubborn, like he was waiting for her to call him a liar. "It's like the dark. It's everywhere. But it's always louder closer to these doors. I asked Renee if she's heard it too, but all she does is laugh or ignore me."

Ghosts. Neither of them said it aloud, but it was impossible not to think it. The house had been abandoned for years, the people who'd gone missing inside of it abandoned too. Nobody liked being forgotten.

Maybe not even old houses and dead people.

Micah sat down with a heavy sigh and rested her back against the door. Theo sat beside her. It was warm against her back, warmer than the rest of the attic at least. She tried to hear the hum of wires or the whisper of voices, but everything was silent. She tilted her head back. Stared up at the crisscross ceiling.

"I think—" she began, when she heard a creak.

They froze. Micah and Theo locked gazes.

If the door creaked again, she couldn't hear it over the heavy beating of her heart. It raced even faster as she slowly leaned forward, off the door. It followed her as she did, the creak stretching into a low whine as the door swung slowly open behind her. It was only a few inches, but it was enough.

Enough to make a decision.

Enough to push it open further.

It was dark inside. And it was empty of ghosts. Empty of everything, really, except a few half-rolled sleeping bags crammed into the corner farthest from the door.

In the middle of the room, though, was a staircase.

At least, she assumed it was. There was a railing and an open space leading down into deeper darkness. But

Micah hadn't seen another staircase in the house besides the one they'd taken to get upstairs, and Theo hadn't mentioned one.

"I'm not going down there."

Theo's voice was quiet but firm. He peered over Micah's shoulder with a frown.

"Why not?"

He shifted his frown from the stairs to her. "Because it's a weird staircase in a creepy room, and I just told you that I heard voices from down there?"

Right. That made sense. Except she was curious. It was like pins and needles in her fingers, traveling up her arms and throughout the rest of her body like electricity. Yes, she knew it was probably a bad idea. A really bad idea. But . . .

"Don't you want to know where it goes?"

Theo shuffled back farther into the safety of the attic. "Not really."

"But what if there's, like, a whole other room down there?"

"Nope."

"What if there's a weird dungeon?"

"Even more of a reason why we shouldn't go down."

"What about buried treasure? You're really going to miss out on gold and jewels because you're scared?"

Okay, so she was reaching. But she really, *really* needed to know. Every new scenario she came up with, however unlikely, only made her eager for the truth.

"I thought you were looking for your grandfather."

Micah winced. It was a clear attempt to change the subject, and her mind, but it didn't make the reprimand sting any less. Before she could respond, there was a soft noise at the edge of her hearing. A mix between low whistling and static.

She crouched lower and leaned farther into the room. The door was such an awkward height that even looking inside meant she was stuck in a half crouch, half squat. Inside the room itself, everything was darker. Even the light of the attic at her back felt farther away.

The dark inside the small, weird room was a darkness Micah felt she might be able to reach out and touch if she focused hard enough.

"Hello?" she whispered into it.

The way she saw it, if something terrifying lived in the dark, it already knew she was there. Talking made her feel a little better.

"Micah, c'mon." Theo sounded agitated, but he also sounded far away. She ignored him.

"Micah?"

She inhaled sharply through her teeth. That hadn't been Theo that time. It wasn't his voice. She kept silent, hoping to hear it again. The voice, so familiar, so close now, didn't disappoint.

"Turtle? That you?"

Poppop's voice filled the tiny room. Micah might have collapsed from relief if she weren't already headed for the stairs, crawling as quickly as she could. The room's poor design—the low walls, the deep slope of the ceiling, the ridiculous staircase—didn't faze her. Poppop was there, somehow. In Finch House, at the bottom of those stairs. All she had to do was reach him. And she would. That was all that was on her mind. No more promises, no more searching for clues.

A hand on her ankle tugged her back before she could reach the railing.

"What're you doing?" Mostly soft-spoken or prone to shrugs since she'd met him, Theo sounded sharper than she'd ever heard him. Fear like barbed wire woven into every word. "You don't know what's down there."

Micah yanked herself free. "My poppop is down there."

He hesitated. Glanced toward the stairs. Then quickly shook his head. "I don't think so. He didn't come in here. And if he did, then maybe . . ."

"No."

There were no maybes. Poppop was downstairs. He'd probably come in through some back entrance or had come looking for her when he saw her bike in the front yard. Either way, she wasn't going to leave just because it was a little scary.

She kept moving until she reached the railing. The stairs weren't very fancy, just a square cut into the floor leading down. And even when she reached them, she couldn't stand. She had to crouch at the top and scoot her way down if she wanted to descend into, well, who knew where?

Theo was right. This far into the room the dark didn't even seem normal anymore. Whatever was beyond the stairs looked filled, like the dark was water that had flooded and consumed everything else.

Maybe it didn't hurt to double-check that Poppop was down there.

Just to be sure.

Micah took a slow, deep breath to calm her racing heart. "Poppop?" she called down.

She stared into the darkness, waiting for an answer. It felt like it was staring back. Watching her. Judging her. Waiting to see what she would do.

"Micah." Theo's voice was a little pleading. "Micah, he's not down there."

She didn't turn to look at him. Instead, she scooted down a step.

chapter seven

Hey, Micah, you left your phone downstairs. Your
mom called and wanted to know if . . ."

Renee trailed off, and the heavy sound of
her footsteps paused. Her legs filled the doorway and
became long, stretching shadows. Then she crouched
and stuck her head inside.

"Creepy room. What're you doing in here?"

Micah, sitting at the top of the stairs, glanced at her
and then back down. It was still silent below. Still dark.
"I—"

"We were just exploring. We're headed back down
now. Right, Micah?" Theo looked at her pointedly. He
was crouched awkwardly in the middle of the room but
still close enough to the door to make a quick escape.

She set her jaw and looked past him to his sister.
"What did my mom say?"

Renee took a second to answer as she looked around, her neck craned sideways to get a better look. "She wanted to know why you weren't answering your phone, where you were, and who I was."

Micah grimaced. She tried not to imagine how many times she'd called or how many texts she'd sent. Her mom was patient, but patience only took her so far before it turned into worry and then solidified into fear.

"You're my one and only baby," she said, usually hugging Micah tight. "I'm always worried about you. And I got you that phone for a reason, so you better answer it when I call."

It didn't matter if Micah had been halfway up a tree or on a bike ride or had forgotten it on the school bus. If her mom's face popped up on her screen, she'd better answer.

With a sigh, she scooted back up to the landing and crawled back toward Theo, Renee, and the attic. She blinked at the fading white light pouring in from the window. Winter sunsets were Poppop's favorite, especially on white sky days. A quiet sunset for a quiet season.

Guilt and unease twisted her stomach into knots as she looked back at the door. Poppop was still down there. But every second spent away from the stairs lessened her certainty. She'd been so sure it was him. She hadn't even wanted to think about any other possibilities. But now, away from the stairs and out of the room, alternate possibilities were all she could think of. That and missing people.

Had they all heard voices at the bottom of the stairs too?

"Micah?"

She turned to Theo. He looked worried. Nothing like the sharp-tongued, leg-yanking boy he'd been in the small attic room. He had saved her, maybe. From the strange darkness if nothing else. She offered up a smile in apology.

"I should call my mom back," she said. "Thanks for, uh . . ."

He nodded when she trailed off. "Renee says you should stay for dinner," he said. "She already mentioned it to your mom."

"Sure," she agreed. "I'll see what she says."

As much as she wasn't looking forward to her mom yelling at her, she hoped she was angry enough to tell her to come home right away. She'd pick her up and maybe she'd get a lecture, but when they got home, Poppop would be there and there'd be dinner on the table. The darkness would be the normal kind, not the type that stared inside her, and she wouldn't have to feel guilty because she hadn't run away scared; she'd just listened to her mom and gone home.

Of course, she did get a lecture. But she also got permission to stay for dinner. So, Micah poked at a plate of gravy-drowned mashed potatoes and pale chicken. She reminded herself that there was nothing to be scared of at Finch House.

"So, Micah, how'd you meet Theo?" Renee asked. She'd cooked, or tried to. Their parents were on a business trip. She'd made it sound like they went on those a lot. "I thought he hadn't left the front yard since we moved in."

"That's where we met, actually. The day before yesterday." Already it felt like ages ago. "I was riding my bike and saw all the stuff on the curb. It looked perfect for networking."

"Networking?" Renee repeated.

Micah explained. She expected teasing or laughter or

confusion, but the older girl only lit up. "I've been finding a bunch of stuff all over the place since we moved in. I've got a box full already."

Without another word, she was out of her seat and out of the kitchen. When she came back, she set a pink shoebox down on the table.

"I don't know what to do with half this stuff, so if you find something in there you like, you can keep it." She glanced at her brother. "You too, I guess."

Micah pushed her plate away and pulled the box close eagerly. Beside her, Theo leaned over to get a better look. Renee had exaggerated. The box wasn't even close to full, but there were a few things to choose from. A fancy golden button that looked like a coin. A shard of glass that caught the light of the chandelier and glittered brightly. A piece of coal.

Micah lifted a faded scrap of yellow and white cloth, the kind that looked like fancy wallpaper, and paused. Underneath it was a key. She reached for it. It didn't look like her house key or any key she'd seen before. This one was small and iron and surprisingly heavy in her palm. Like the knocker on the front door, a small bird perched on the length of it like it was a branch.

"What's this for?" she asked.

Renee shrugged. "Dunno. I tried a couple doors, but none of them worked."

Micah curled her fingers around it. She wanted it with a suddenness that startled her. She felt her heartbeat in her palm like it was laying claim to the key with every beat.

Mine. Mine. Mine.

"I can have it, right?"

Renee had already said as much, but she wanted to make sure. Still, she didn't know if a lack of permission would have stopped her from taking it.

Renee agreed. When Micah was finally able to take her attention off the key, she turned to Theo. "Find anything?"

He held up a long chain. A small silver pocket watch swung back and forth from the end of it. It was broken. When he flicked open the front, both hands spun wildly.

They pawed through the rest of the box, showing each other straggling tassels and old pennies, until dinner was over. By the time they were done, Micah felt almost normal. Maybe Finch House was too. A normal house, same as the rest of the houses on the street. Maybe there were no ghosts in its depths. No decades-old missing people in the attic.

She couldn't quite bring herself to believe that, though.

Theo walked her to the door. Neither of them talked, but it wasn't quiet. The house creaked around them, old bones and busy pipes.

Micah meant to say goodbye. She meant to thank him for riding around town searching for Poppop with her and not leaving her on her own in the attic. Instead, she said, "How can you live here? Aren't you scared you're going to disappear?"

Because she was. Even while she ate and laughed and joked. Even as she stood in the hallway with the front door so close by, anxiety crept its way through her like blood in her veins. Part of her was so sure she was already stuck. What if she couldn't leave? What if Finch House didn't let her?

She studied Theo's face, hoping to see her own fears reflected back at her. He was good at holding it together. But Micah was stubborn. She stared until she was nearly glaring, closely enough that she caught the way he bit the inside of his lip. His eyes flickered past her, over her shoulder to the door where the outside waited.

"You should go," he said.

"Not until you answer me."

His eyes met hers. After a moment he shrugged. "Maybe I'm a little scared. But there's nowhere else to go. Like you said, I live here."

She wanted to shake him. Or call his parents and tell them that they should move. Or scream loudly enough that she scared away whatever made the darkness in Finch House feel so prying, so thick, like it was smothering her and cutting her open at the same time.

Mostly, though, she just wanted to go home. All the guilt in the world couldn't compare to the relief she felt at just the thought of it. Even her new house had to be better than here.

"I'm sorry," she said. It felt like both the right and wrong thing to say to someone who could disappear at any time. She rubbed her arm, slightly chilled so close to the door, and let her hand trail down to Nana's bracelet and the small charm that dangled from it.

Well.

The small charm that *should* have dangled from it, if the bracelet she'd worn every day for a year was still clasped around her wrist. But it wasn't.

Micah sucked in a sharp breath and waited for panic

to settle in. It didn't. Instead came dread like ice water in her belly.

She'd lost her bracelet, sure, but she knew exactly where she'd be able to find it. And the house knew it too. The stairs leading up to the attic creaked low and long, though no one walked up or down them.

She locked eyes with Theo. Watched something change in them when she said, "I have to go back upstairs."

chapter eight

Had she lost it, or had the house taken it?

That was the question that propelled Micah forward.

Up the stairs.

Into the attic.

Inside the tiny room.

She'd worn the bracelet every day since Nana put it on her wrist with skinny, shaking fingers. She'd taken it off only once, to go swimming with her neighbor, Hannah, and only then because Mom warned her that the chlorine might tarnish it. And still her mom had had to help her; the clasp was too stubborn to take off on her own.

She paused, crouched in front of the attic room's stairs. Her heart hammered against her chest as if it wanted to get out and lead her down.

The clasp. She hadn't undone it, *couldn't* undo it on her own. Which meant that she had her answer.

She hadn't lost the bracelet at all.

The house had just needed an excuse to get her back upstairs.

She could almost hear Nana's voice in her ear, feel her tickling hands as she rubbed her arms, reassuring her whenever she was afraid of something, whether it was a scary movie or a dance recital.

It's okay to be scared, but you've got a whole well of courage in your belly. You get too scared, you know what you do? Just take a deep old breath and draw up a bucketful of that courage.

"What if it runs out?" Micah had asked. She asked it now, too, in a whisper.

It won't. It's yours for whenever you need it.

The memory calmed her. She clicked on her phone's flashlight and turned toward the stairs.

"Wait!"

The word burst from Theo, sitting beside her and staring miserably into the darkness, suddenly enough that she nearly dropped her phone. "You don't know what's down there."

"I guess I'm going to find out." She turned to him. "Are you coming?"

Doubt flickered across his face. She could tell how much he wanted to protest, how much he wanted to stop her. And she understood. Hadn't she just asked him if he was afraid of disappearing in this strange house?

Without waiting for his answer, Micah turned back to the gaping mouth of the stairs and started creeping down.

Cold overtook her in a rush, a breeze that shouldn't have existed in an attic. With it came so many emotions. Fear. Confusion. Rage as sudden as a camera flash in the dark. None of them were Micah's—at least she didn't think so. She felt detached from them, like she was wading through them as much as she was wading through the darkness. It made it hard to feel Theo's presence behind her, even as he rambled.

"I really don't get why we're going down here. If you lost your bracelet, it would be on the stairs we already passed, not at the bottom."

She ignored him. He continued.

"I really think we should go back. Anything could be down there. We don't even know where 'there' is."

That was the terrifying part. But it was also, she thought, part of the fun. A bit of excitement to go along with the fear the way it did whenever she waited in line for a roller coaster—just enough to keep her moving forward.

Somewhere between the first step and whichever she was on now, her brain had shut itself off. Fear had too. Something was driving her, coaxing her downstairs, and it was more than just her curiosity, though it tingled in the back of her neck and buzzed in both ears just like it.

"You don't have to come with me, you know."

"I know. I just feel like maybe—"

For a moment Micah thought he'd just stopped talking. She crept forward a few more steps, wood whining beneath her. She paused when she didn't hear the sound echo behind her.

"Theo?" If he was going to turn around, he could have at least warned her. "Are you still here?"

It *felt* like he was. There was a weight in the darkness his size and shape behind her, even if it made no noise on the stairs. All she had to do was turn around to know for sure. She tightened her grip on her phone. The light wavered as she started turning.

"I'm still here."

Micah froze.

Not Theo, her mind warned.

The voice was too soft. There and not there, like someone was whispering in her ear and calling from the bottom of the stairs at the same time. Like the voice had come from the house or the stairs or the darkness itself.

"Theo?" she whispered again.

Nothing. No Theo. No voice. Not even a breath.

The silence was suffocating. Where the undercurrent of ever-present noise had been a comfort, silence wrapped itself around her and held on tight. Too tight to breathe deeply. Too tight to access any of the courage in her belly. It squeezed and squeezed and *squeezed* . . .

"You're almost there, Micah."

Micah sucked in a breath and raced back upstairs on her hands and knees.

She ignored every trip and stumble, every banged shin. Nothing about this was fun anymore. The roller coaster had broken down, and she was *not* getting on it. Escape was the only thought in her head now. Escape and light and getting as far as possible from the voice that seemed to fill the stairwell—the steps themselves, the wood they were made of, and every gap between them.

Back on the landing, she crawled her way toward the door. Theo was nowhere. She couldn't think about him now anyway. Not whether he'd left her or if he was hurt or if he and the voice were somehow the same. She scrambled for the door as fast as she could, praying that it would open.

It did, and Micah tumbled out of the room and back into the attic. She slammed the door shut behind her and leaned hard against it to catch her breath. Her eyes slid shut in relief. Her head pounded to the same beat as her heart. Her knees hurt. But each new breath brought gratitude.

When she opened her eyes, though, gratitude fled.

She turned slowly to her left. Then her right. The attic she'd been in only a few minutes ago—dusty and empty and dimly lit—was gone. Instead, a bright orange couch covered in yellow flowers was shoved against the window next to two beanbag chairs. A foosball table stood on wobbly legs in the middle of the room, surrounded by stuffed animals and action figures Micah had never seen before.

And staring at her, mid–toy pickup, was a girl about Renee's age with huge, feathery blond hair, wide-legged jeans, and a deep frown. She picked up the nearest toy and straightened up with a sigh.

"Great," she said. "Another one for me to babysit."

chapter nine

O kay," the girl said. "Let's make this quick. My name's Callie. Yes, this is still the same house. No, I don't know how to get out or why you're here." Callie grabbed another stuffed animal, the sad-looking bear joining the zoo already filling her arms. "Any other questions?"

Micah had plenty. Starting with "Are you a ghost?" and ending with "Have you seen Theo or Poppop?"

Callie was good at multitasking. Releasing the toys in her arms into a toy chest, she kicked a beanbag chair back into place. "Can't answer the ghost thing. Not because I don't want to but because I don't know, and I try not to think about that kind of thing too much. It's pretty easy, too, considering the mess." She gestured to the attic. Despite her cleaning, there still seemed to be toys everywhere. "This babysitting job was supposed to be a one-night deal, but here I am."

She frowned faintly, eyeing Micah. "And here you are. Weird clothes. I'd ask where you're from"—when Micah opened her mouth to answer, the older girl shook her head—"but I don't want to know. Best for both of us, probably. Now, who'd you say you were looking for again?"

Micah explained, trying to describe Poppop to the best of her ability. She brightened when she remembered the phone in her hand, still shining dimly, and pulled up a picture of the two of them together. She'd taken it the other morning, as they headed out networking. Poppop was leaned over into her seat, the brim of his Navy hat brushing against her curls, his smile wide and toothy, his beard more white than gray against his brown skin. She held it out toward Callie. The older girl recoiled, then bent forward hesitantly.

"That's far out," she whispered. When Micah looked at her, confused, she shook her head. "Sorry, I've never seen him. That's probably a good thing around here, though."

Micah put her phone away with a sigh. "What do you mean?"

"I told you, there's no way out. Or back. Or whatever. You fell through, and now you're stuck like the rest of us."

Micah frowned. "But I didn't fall. I was just trying to get out of that weird room, and then I opened the door and—"

"No."

Callie's voice was soft. She'd stopped cleaning for a moment to look at Micah, and Micah wished she hadn't. Even though she wasn't a grown-up, she had the same sad eyes grown-ups got when they were about to tell you bad news.

"I didn't mean actually fall. It's what the rest of us call how we got here—falling through. Because there's no real explanation. It's just like falling into a gap in the world. None of us know how long we've been here or when we got here. Every day feels the same but also just different enough that we know it's not." She sighed. "I've cleaned up these toys a million times, but as far as I know, it's still 1977. My car's still parked out front, a cute little Bug, and I'm still going out to see *Saturday Night Fever* with my friends this weekend."

Micah tried not to stare and tried not to let fear grip her. She failed at both. Callie had been here for such a long time—she was even older than her mom. She was one of the disappeared people.

And now so was Micah.

Finch House had just decided to collect her and everyone else like seashells at the beach.

"Hey." Micah glanced up. "Don't look so upset. I'll try to introduce you to some people," Callie said, abandoning the rest of the mess and heading for the door. "It's easier, being around other people in the beginning. Trust me, I—"

She cut off abruptly as she walked through the wall. Not the door. *The wall.* Micah stared and then decided she didn't want to chance it herself. She swung open the door instead, prepared to hurry after Callie, but Callie was nowhere in sight. She couldn't even hear her voice anymore. There was only the small landing the attic was on and the main stairs directly in front of her.

There was nowhere else to go, so Micah went down.

"Callie?" she called.

The hallway, at least, looked normal. There was a different colored rug cushioning her footsteps, but it hadn't changed as drastically as the attic had. The thought was reassuring even as the hallway seemed to get longer and longer until it felt like she had been walking forever. Micah tried some of the handles to the rooms she passed, but none of them opened. And she couldn't hear or see Callie anywhere.

"Theo? Poppop?"

Maybe they'd fallen through too. Or maybe all of this was a dream. Maybe she'd fallen down the stairs and hit her head and was, right at this very second, asleep in bed with an ice pack on her head and a blanket covering her. The thought warmed her just as a rush of cold air blew through the hall like someone had left the window open. Except Micah didn't see any windows. And instead of rushing past her, the cold air rushed around her.

Circling her, gathering her up in itself like the videos of tornadoes she'd seen on TV.

"H-hello?" she called out through chattering teeth.

It was incorrect to say that nothing answered her. Finch House did, in its own way. A whisper in the corner. The long creak of settling wood. The shifting darkness like someone flicking a light switch on and off.

She tried to get away from it. The cold, the noise. But it only followed her, or else she took a wrong turn and ended up back in the middle of it. Left turns were wrong. Right turns too. Walking straight ahead or going farther downstairs didn't help either. The house moved as she did, shifting forward and back, left and right and upside down until Micah felt like she had after a trip on the Tilt-A-Whirl at the county fair.

She startled at the sudden vibration in her pocket, then quickly took her phone out. She had service! Someone was calling her! Her heart lifted at the sight of her mom's picture on the screen. She answered quickly, shoving the phone against her ear.

"Mom! I'm sorry, I—"

"Micah? I've been waiting . . ." Her mom's voice trailed off into static, every other word distorted and garbled like she was speaking through a mouthful of marbles. "When . . . have . . . *nighttime* . . . getting worried . . ."

"Mom?" she called. "Mom?"

The phone beeped. Slowly, Micah took it from her ear. She'd lost signal, or it had died. It didn't matter which. All that mattered was that she was alone.

Again.

Completely.

The world was only two things now: Micah and the darkness.

She wasn't normally afraid of the dark, but this was different. She thought she understood what Theo meant now. How deeply it stared. How quiet everything seemed.

She felt the ache of tears in her throat even before she felt the fat, wet drops on her eyelashes. She wanted to be brave and keep charging through the halls, daring anything or anyone to mess with her, but she was tired. All the courage inside her felt like the last bit of juice in a Capri Sun, but she couldn't taste it no matter how hard she squeezed the juice pack or sucked on the straw.

Maybe Callie was right.

Maybe she really was stuck and Poppop was gone and her mom would wait, wait, wait for them both to come back. If she waited too long, she'd probably move to the new house alone and shove all Micah's stuff into a closet the way she had Nana's.

She leaned against the wall and sank down until she could wrap her arms around her legs. Finch House was so quiet that her sniffs echoed as she buried her face in her knees and let herself cry.

Just for a few minutes, she promised herself. Just a few minutes and she could try to find her courage again.

Micah Robinson cried for longer than a few minutes. But sometimes you need to.

chapter ten

A re you lost?" Finch House asked.

It had the voice of a little girl, soft and worried. The voice of someone who might help her.

But Micah didn't lift her head. She didn't trust voices that didn't belong to bodies anymore. All they'd done was taken her bracelet—which she still hadn't found—and led her to dark, deserted hallways in parts of the house she wasn't sure actually existed.

But then a hand rested itself lightly on her knee. And she felt *warmth*.

She dared a look up. And stared straight into dark eyes that could have mirrored her own.

The girl stepped back with a soft smile, and Micah lifted her head fully to get a better look at her. She was about her own height and age, maybe a little older, with dark twists on either side of her head and a soft, careful smile. Her dress looked old, too old even for the vintage store her mom liked to go to.

"Are you lost?" the girl asked again.

Micah nodded, rubbing her eyes. "Do you know how to get out of here?"

"No," she admitted. "I'm Jenn."

"Micah."

Jenn took a seat next to her, close enough that their shoulders touched. Again, warmth seeped through Micah, such a difference from the chill of the house that she shivered. She hadn't touched Callie, so she didn't know if this girl was a ghost too, if all ghosts felt this warm. Maybe she was Micah's kind of lost, too, new to the house to be anything but alive and looking for a way out.

Besides, Micah didn't want to think too hard about what it meant if the only people in the house with her were ghostly.

"I'm looking for people," she said, hoping she could help more than Callie had been able to. "A boy and an old man. Have you seen them?"

She gave the best descriptions of Theo and Poppop

that she could, but Jenn shook her head. "I've seen lots of boys. Not that boy, though. And no old men."

Micah nodded slowly, ignoring the tears that threatened. Poppop and Theo were gone. But for now, at least, she wasn't alone. "How long have you been here?"

A dark cloud passed over Jenn's face, but it was gone when Micah blinked. "I don't know." Before Micah could offer up the year, she continued. "You feel it, don't you? How being here even for a little while feels like forever?"

She did.

Everything felt stretched, like someone had turned time into slime and kept pulling it longer and longer, thinner and thinner.

"I have an idea," Jenn said suddenly, hopping up. "I'll give you a tour. You can still ask me questions, but it beats just sitting here. C'mon," she said, holding out a hand when Micah hesitated. "At least if we get lost, we're lost together, right?"

Together.

Micah took the other girl's hand and nodded. She was still curious, of course, and it was always easier to explore with a friend. Even somewhere that changed as often as Finch House did.

Jenn was a good guide. She reminded Micah of the real estate agents on some of the shows she watched with her mom, taking her through each room and telling her everything she knew about it. Micah tried not to think about how long she'd have to be there to know as much about Finch House as Jenn seemed to.

"This house is really cool," Jenn said excitedly, leading her down a hall. "I mean besides"—she gestured around them—"everything. It was built in the early 1900s, I think maybe 1905, by Leroy Finch."

With its long carpets in the hall and floral wallpaper, the candle-like wall lights and gold-framed paintings everywhere, Finch House really did look like it belonged to a different time.

"It was one of the biggest houses around here for a while. Even one of the newspapers made a big deal about it since it was built by a Black man."

"It was?"

Jenn beamed. "Yup!"

"But I thought—"

"It was lost during the Great Depression. Taken by the bank and sold," she continued with a frown. "And then the neighborhood changed. Only some people could buy houses on this street and in this area. No one else was allowed."

Micah nodded. Poppop had told her a few stories about his childhood, even if he had never mentioned his sister in any of them.

"How do you know all that?" Hours of googling hadn't told her a single thing.

"Oh, you learn lots of stuff living here. It's not important," Jenn said quickly. "Look!" She pointed down the hall. "The house is welcoming you."

Lights turned on as they passed, the warm yellow glow banishing the darkness and the shadows. The whispers that filled the halls faded. The whole house, which had steadily felt like it had been boxing her in, felt like it had decided to expand to its full size, like it was taking a deep breath.

Reflexively, Micah took one too. "Does it do that for everyone?"

Jenn shot her a small smile. "No," she said. "Not for everyone."

Micah nodded, relaxing slightly. "Can we go up to the tower?"

She remembered Renee's story about the boy who

had disappeared up there. If he'd vanished from there, maybe she could too. Only in her case, vanishing would mean going back to the real world. At least, she hoped so.

Jenn glanced at her. "The tower?"

"The turret. I've always wanted to see the view from up there." That wasn't even a lie. "Have you been inside? Is it just a room full of windows, or is there—"

"There's nothing up there," the other girl interrupted. "It's empty. And locked."

"If it's locked, how do you know it's empty?"

"I just do, okay?" Jenn frowned. "Trust me. There's nothing for you up there."

Confused, Micah opened her mouth to ask why but shut it after a quick glance at Jenn. All her early excitement over showing the house was gone. Instead, she looked upset. Angry. And it felt like Micah's fault.

"That's okay," she said as they headed downstairs. "I don't need to see it right now."

Micah was already thinking of ways to get to the turret on her own, or other places like the stairs that had the potential to send her back, when she and Jenn rounded the corner. She paused.

There were people! Walking up and down the stairs, talking to one another in the halls, sitting on couches and in long, fancy reclining chairs or at the dining room table. New people must have been normal for them; none of them even looked her way.

"Shouldn't we go talk to them?" Micah asked, hesitating as Jenn started leading her away. "They might have seen Theo or Poppop or—"

"They won't help you."

"What? Why not?"

Jenn shrugged. "Most of them don't like new kids. It reminds them of when they first got here. Don't worry," she said, looping her arm with Micah's. "I like you. You're better off with me anyway."

Micah wasn't sure how much of the house Jenn had shown her so far, but it felt like a lot. Most of the doors were locked, and she refused to check if she could walk through walls or not, but there was still so much to see. Sitting rooms, play rooms, music rooms, offices. It felt like too many rooms, even for Finch House. Walking between them felt like going back and forward in time. Already, Micah had seen typewriters and old-school radios in rooms right across the hall from ones with flat-screen TVs and gaming computers.

In a room with a fireplace nearly as tall as her, Micah drifted away from Jenn, over to a familiar-looking half door. It was the same as the others she'd seen. Same paint, same keyhole. Still no way to open it.

"They're the only things we can't walk through, you know."

Micah startled at a voice that wasn't Jenn's. A red-haired boy had appeared next to her from nowhere. He was small, too young even for fifth grade, and the bottoms of his shoes lit up bright green when he shuffled in place.

"They look like part of the wall, but you try to walk through and . . . nothing." He shrugged, still looking at the door. "It's kinda nice. Makes me feel normal."

"Do you think they all lead to the same place?" Was this where the stairs in the attic would lead, somewhere as normal as this room? Or did they all lead someplace different, have their own destinations in mind?

If the redhead heard her question, he didn't answer it. Instead, he stepped closer to her, lowering his voice. There was no warmth around him, she noticed absently.

Nothing that cut through the house's chill. If anything, she felt colder the closer he stood. "I don't know where they go. But I know you shouldn't stay with her," he whispered. "She's not—"

"Making friends?"

Both startled at the sound of Jenn's voice. She walked over to them with a wide smile, looking from Micah to the redheaded boy. "I guess I should stop rambling about this place and let you explore on your own, huh?"

"No, it's okay," Micah assured her. "I like learning about Finch House. Especially this . . . version of it."

There was nothing renovated about it, like in the version Theo lived in, but nothing overly historical, either. It felt like a mix of all the different houses Finch House had been over the years based on whoever lived there. Like it had absorbed parts of each one. Wherever Micah was, it felt like the core of Finch House.

She turned back to the boy. "Hey, have you—" She blinked when nothing stood in his place but cold air.

"Did you see where he went?" she asked, turning back to Jenn.

The other girl shrugged. "The little kids here can be shy sometimes. What were you going to ask him?"

"Just if he'd seen Poppop or Theo. I was hoping . . ."
Micah trailed off with a sigh and automatically brought
her hand to her wrist to twist her bracelet charm between
her fingers. She faltered when she met empty space,
remembering that even her bracelet was gone.

Was this it? Was she one of the missing now, lost or
left behind, stuck in some version of Finch House that
was as endless as space?

Would Poppop, wherever he was, forget her like he'd
forgotten his sister?

Would her mom?

She didn't want to be forgotten. It sounded like a ter-
rible, unmaking thing.

"Hey." Jenn's voice was soft. "Are you okay?"

She reached for Micah's hand, and only then did
Micah realize how tightly she'd curled her fingers into
each palm. She relaxed slowly, the bite of her nails tingling in her hands.

"Don't freak out, okay? I know it's scary, but if they're
here, we'll find them. It might take a little while, but"—
she shrugged, giving Micah a smile—"time doesn't really
mean much here."

That was what she was afraid of. Still, Micah fixed her

lips into the best smile she could. She let Jenn squeeze her hand reassuringly before she let go.

"You know this place best," she said. "Where do you think we should start?"

All she needed was a plan. Even here, in this liminal house, a plan was what would work. A plan would keep the scared parts of herself from curling up in corners and the curious parts of herself from sticking her head into every closet.

"Top to bottom can't hurt, right? Mama always said that was the best way to clean, so it's probably the best way to search, too. Tour part two."

"Sure," Micah said. She didn't think that was the best advice in a house that constantly changed itself, but Jenn knew this place and she didn't. Besides, it was a beginning. And a beginning was always better than nothing.

Searching for missing people in a house full of them was not nearly as easy as it sounded.

For one, Finch House was huge. Walking through it once had been enough, but as they searched, it seemed even more confusing than before. Hallways suddenly became dead ends. Doors that Micah remembered being open were now locked. It felt like Finch House had thrown them into the worst game of hide-and-seek Micah had ever played.

Even worse, no one wanted to talk.

The moment the girls approached anyone, they disappeared. Literally. One second a group of kids and teenagers could be chatting, and the next the room was as empty as if they'd never been there. Micah tried not to take it personally, but there didn't feel like any other way to take it.

Eventually, searching in focused silence felt like too much. Her heart beat too fast at every shadow that looked like it could be Poppop, and her brain wouldn't stop asking questions. What time was it now? How long could she stay without becoming a ghost if she wasn't already one? Had Theo gone back upstairs, or was he here, looking for her just as hard as she was looking for him and Poppop?

She had no answers, not even any clues. It all made her stomach ache.

"Can I ask you something, Jenn? You can say no."

"You'd be the only one who's asked me anything in a

long time," she said, and Micah wondered if she had any friends here at all. "Ask away."

"Do you remember what it was like to *not* be here?"

Jenn paused. She was quiet long enough that Micah thought she'd decided not to answer after all. But when she spoke, her voice was softer. Faraway, like it was stuck in her own memories.

"Yes and no," she said. "I can remember most of it. Dust on my clothes walking home from school, how ice cream made my teeth ache. But all that feels less real than here does. Like how a dream gets when you wake up, all blurry and strange at the edges."

She looked at Micah. She seemed sad, even with the half smile she wore. Her eyes were darker without their usual spark, and even the air around her flickered colder.

"You want to know what I remember the most?"

Micah nodded.

"I remember my little brother. He wasn't that little, I guess, only a year younger than me, but we did everything together. Climbed trees. Chased chickens. Had contests to see who could swing the highest. It was me, of course."

She laughed. "Elijah liked to run. He'd run everywhere." Her voice dropped until it didn't sound like she was talking to Micah at all anymore. "Some days that's all I can remember of before. Elijah's face when he ran, wind in his hair and dirt kicked up by his heels."

Micah nodded, but she wasn't listening anymore. Not really. She was studying Jenn—her round jaw and dark eyes and brown skin. The small mole on her left cheek and the other two up by her right eye. She compared her in her head to the blurry girl in the picture as best she could, and to Poppop.

Poppop, whose actual name was Elijah.

Poppop, whose sister, like Jenn, had gone missing in Finch House.

"Jenn," she said slowly, "I think you might know my poppop."

"I already told you I haven't seen him. I think I'd notice—"

"I think he's your brother," Micah blurted out. She didn't know how to make it less of a shock for both of them. "Just . . ." All grown up. "Just older."

Jenn stared at her. She shook her head, but it didn't stop the smile from slowly spreading across her face. "Elijah is here? And grown up? And you . . . ?" Her eyes widened. "And you! If you're his granddaughter—his *granddaughter*—then that makes me your—"

"My great-aunt."

"Right. Okay."

Jenn stared. Micah stared back. Warmth pulsed around them. The lights in the house seemed brighter. They were so bright that her eyes watered.

Both girls launched themselves forward at the same time, crashing into a hug that filled Micah with warmth and an odd happiness, the same kind she got when she found the last piece of a puzzle or finished her math homework.

"What now?" she asked when they pulled away. She could almost see the gears turning in her great-aunt's head, everything still falling into place. She looked far away.

"We find him," Jenn said simply.

She headed down the latest hallway and straight for the stairs. Micah quickened her own steps to keep up.

She shivered as the temperature around them changed. Every few steps she walked into a cold patch, cold enough that goose bumps rippled up and down her arms. She tried to stick close to Jenn and the warmth she gave off, but even that flickered on and off, hot as fire one moment, freezing cold the next.

She'd just taken her first step off the landing and onto the stairs when the air around her . . . moved. There was no other way for her to describe it—it was too quick to pinpoint. One second she was stepping down, and the next she was being yanked sideways, the flutter in her belly the same kind she got on roller coasters.

She stumbled, catching herself on the railing before she could fall into Jenn and send them both headfirst down the stairs.

"Jenn, did you feel—" She paused. Not just because she didn't know if she was allowed to call her great-aunt by her first name anymore but also because she was no longer on the stairs in front of her.

"Jenn?" she called again.

Micah turned around, a feeling of déjà vu like a pit in her stomach. She craned her head up to get a better look at both sides of the landing. Jenn was nowhere in sight.

Finch House was different too. Gone were the old paintings and faded floral wallpaper. Now there were a few framed photos on the wall that felt familiar, black-and-white landscapes of mountains and pyramids and lakes. Even the air felt different, warm for winter but not the skin-deep warmth she'd felt around Jenn. And the weird darkness was back. Crammed under doorways and curled up in corners like it was sleepy or waiting.

Tentative relief filled Micah, and she took the stairs two at a time, eager to see if she was somehow back in the Finch House that she knew, the Finch House where Theo lived and hopefully still was. She rounded the corner into the entryway and immediately bumped into something hard enough to send her stumbling backward.

She caught herself before she could fall, lifting her head to see what she'd bumped into. Theo stared back at her, wide-eyed and openmouthed.

Looking like he'd just seen, and run into, a ghost.

chapter eleven

Y ou're not dead!" he blurted out.

Micah really hoped not. "I don't think so."

"But you—I mean I saw you. You just . . ." He waved his hands frantically, his interpretation of what she assumed was her disappearance. "And then I thought maybe you just went down, so I went to the door at the bottom of the stairs, but it still wouldn't open and—"

"Theo."

"I've been looking all over the place. You weren't anywhere! Your mom even called Renee, but I didn't know what to tell her and I'm really bad at stalling. It's like lying but worse—"

"*Theo.*"

"—so I asked if you could spend the night because, you know, winter break, and also I had no clue if my house had swallowed you or how I would tell your mom that, especially since she did *not* sound happy. I think maybe you're grounded now? But she did say you could stay over since you're moving soon. I didn't know you were moving, but—"

"Theo!"

Micah had never heard him say so much, and now, when she was trying to figure out how she'd even gotten back, was not the time to deal with his newfound talkative side. "Just give me a second, okay?"

He paused with visible effort, shutting his mouth to look her over. Micah ignored him. Instead, she took a deep breath, slowly looking around as she checked in with herself. There was her jacket, hanging on the hook by the door. There was her heart, slowly returning to its normal rhythm.

And there was Theo, safe in the normal version of his house, still staring at her.

First carefully, then suspiciously. "You're not a ghost, are you?"

"No," she said firmly. "I just ran into you." She decided to leave out the fact that she might have met a few.

The suspicion didn't leave his face, so when he stuck

out a finger to poke her, she let him. They both relaxed when it pressed lightly into her shoulder.

"So, where did you go? What happened?"

Micah shook her head. She didn't know how to explain it. "How long was I gone?"

He took his phone out of his pocket. "I dunno, maybe twenty minutes?"

"Twenty minutes?"

That was impossible. She'd walked through Finch House twice with Jenn and who knew how many times on her own when she'd been looking for a way out. It felt like it had been days since she'd last seen Theo, not minutes.

"Micah?" Theo pulled her out of her thoughts. "Tell me what happened."

"I don't know. We were going downstairs, and then you were gone, and I . . . I was here, in Finch House, looking for you. And for Poppop."

"Did you find him?"

She shook her head. "No. We were about to go looking, but everything got all . . . twisted . . . and then I was back here."

She rubbed her eyes. They burned a bit, like she'd been

staring at a screen for too long. "Can I have some water?"

Theo nodded, leading her to the kitchen. Everything felt familiar as she watched him move around, grabbing cups from a cabinet and a pitcher from the fridge. Paprika was even still asleep in her bed.

She chugged the water gratefully when he handed it to her, the cold clearing her head and relaxing something in her that moving through time and space had agitated.

Theo refilled her cup. "Are you really moving?"

"What?"

"When your mom called and I was trying to stall for you, she said you were moving."

"Oh." Micah sighed. She hated the reminder. "Yeah. Just me and Mom. And even if—*when*—I find Poppop, once we're gone, he'll still be all alone. . . ."

She trailed off, frowning into her cup. After a moment, she sat up straight, a sudden thought making her gasp. "But maybe he doesn't have to be."

Theo eyed her warily. "What do you mean?"

"I mean if I'm here . . . if I can leave that version of Finch House, then maybe Jenn can too! I can go back and bring her with me and she can stay with Poppop."

She nodded to herself, oblivious to Theo as she turned

and started heading back upstairs. "It'll be perfect. It won't even matter that I broke my promise because Jenn won't be missing anymore, and Poppop won't have any reason to be afraid of this place."

Theo hurried behind her. "Where are you going? Who's Jenn? Did you not hear me say that your mom was worried about you? You can at least send her a text or—"

She whirled around, nearly losing her footing on the step. "She's Poppop's sister! My great-aunt. She's been stuck here for so long; I can't just *leave* her."

"But you can't go back! You don't even know how you got there. Or here. Going back is like stepping into a monster's mouth after it spit you out."

She frowned. Part of her knew he was right. It was the part that couldn't shake off how alone she'd felt in the halls, in the dark, or how strangely everyone had reacted to her and Jenn. But the rest of her was stubborn. She'd broken a promise to Poppop, but now she had the chance to make it right. To make it better.

If she brought Jenn back, Poppop would *have* to forgive her.

Micah continued her way up the stairs until she was

standing in front of the attic door. She put her hand on the knob. "You don't have to come in with me."

"I know. Just like you don't have to go in there. You don't *have* to."

"Yes, I do."

"She's already gone, Micah!"

If she could exist in both Finch Houses—get to see the house now and all the houses it had been before like peeking behind a curtain—then she knew Jenn could too. There was something different about her compared to the other kids Micah had met. They'd felt like ghosts, like shadows of whoever they'd been before they came to Finch House. Even Micah had felt out of sorts. But Jenn had only ever felt solid.

Real in a way that nothing else in Finch House seemed to be.

"Not if I bring her back."

Micah started to open the door, but Theo moved quickly. He was between her and the door before she could blink, her hand at her side, stinging more from surprise than pain where he'd slapped it away.

She glared at him. "What are you doing?"

"Trying to stop you." He bit his lip. Hair was falling

into his face, and his cheeks were red, flushed like he'd been running. "Is it working?"

"*No*. It's just annoying. Get out of my way."

"Just listen to me. Please. I saw more . . . I saw more of those kid-shaped shadows while you were gone." He grimaced. "*Ghosts*. And they've been, well, not exactly talking but—"

"Great. Ghosts. I saw them too. Even talked to some of them." She tried not to focus on how wild that sounded. "So, if you're done, can you just"—she tried to get around him without barreling straight into him—"move?"

"It's a bad idea, Micah."

"You can say 'I told you so' later if something happens to me, but right now I'm—"

"It's my house," Theo said suddenly. He still looked nervous, but his jaw was set and his eyes were hard. "It's my house now, and if I don't want you to go into my attic, then you can't." He took a deep breath. His hands shook a little, but he didn't move and he didn't stop looking at her. "You should go home."

Home.

Home, where Poppop was supposed to be.

Home, where she only had a few days left to actually

spend with him before some other house was supposed to magically become her new home.

Home, she realized, didn't actually mean anything if her poppop wasn't there, or if he never wanted to talk to her again because she'd broken her promise. *He* was what she would miss when they left. Not her room or her tree house in the backyard or the way she could hear the mailman at the mailbox all the way from the kitchen.

It was Poppop she hated leaving. Which meant she couldn't leave him now, all alone. Especially not if he had a sister she could bring back to keep him company. To make him happy. Not even if it meant shoving Theo out of the way in his own house.

"What if the house swallowed Renee?" she asked, holding his gaze. "Would you just sit in your room pretending it didn't happen, waiting for your parents to get home? Would you not want to help her?"

Theo shook his head, more like he was trying to drown out her voice than answer her question. It made her suddenly, ridiculously angry.

"Are you that much of a coward?" she snapped. "That much of a baby that you wouldn't even try to help her?"

He flinched, but she didn't back down. "Maybe you wouldn't even *care*—"

Pain gripped her tight around the middle. It was worse than the worst stomachache she'd ever had. Worse than the time Kerry Baker accidentally hit her in the face with a dodgeball during gym.

There was a rope wrapped tight around her stomach, and someone or something was tugging on it, trying to pull her back down. Or she was a light and someone was flicking her on and off. Or she might explode right there in the middle of the hallway for no good reason.

In a panic, she reached for Theo, holding tight to his sweater-covered wrist.

She didn't mean to, really. But he was there, and she was scared, and if the house was going to swallow her up again, she didn't want to be alone this time.

She wasn't.

And she wouldn't have been even if Theo hadn't been beside her, his nails dug deep into the hand she gripped him with like holding on tight was going to keep either of them where they were. All the anger and frustration and hurt got lost in the upside-down, inside-out movement.

When the pain and dizziness passed and Micah's eyes

focused, Jenn was standing in front of them.

"You're back!" her great-aunt said excitedly.

She rushed toward Micah in a flurry of cold air and wrapped her in a hug. It didn't feel like the last time they'd hugged. There was some sort of barrier between them now, thick as air but still noticeable. Like Jenn was only solid in theory. She let go before Micah could figure out what was wrong.

"Do you know how much energy it took to bring you back? Even more than it took to bring Elijah here in the first place, and that was a lot! I thought I'd have to siren song you again."

Micah stared at her. "What are you talking about?"

Jenn laughed. "You know"—she cleared her throat— "*Turtle*," she said in perfect imitation of Poppop's voice.

Micah shivered. "What . . . ?"

Her great-aunt smiled. "Don't you get it? Now we can all be here, together, and no one will get left behind."

"But . . ." Micah struggled to put her racing thoughts into words. "But I was already coming back to get you. You could come home with us and—"

"I can't go anywhere, Micah," Jenn interrupted, shaking her head. "That's the whole thing; Finch House is my home. Besides, I didn't need you to save me. You can't even save yourself. If I hadn't found you, you'd still be wandering the halls looking for Elijah." She perked up, smiling brightly. "But it doesn't matter anymore! It's your home now too. Both your homes."

"Oh!" she exclaimed suddenly. "I almost forgot."

Jenn held out her hand. In it was a thin silver brace-let, a heart-shaped charm dangling from the end.

"This is yours."

chapter twelve

Micah snatched her bracelet back with a gasp and stared at the girl in front of her with wide eyes.

It was one thing to hear someone admit to something and quite another to see the evidence. The voice, the thing that had terrified her in the dark, that had snatched her away, wasn't Finch House.

It was this girl.

It was Jenn.

Micah had so many questions. She usually did. But this time, none came out; all she could do was stare. This wasn't the same girl who'd found her crying in a dark hall and became her friend. This wasn't the same girl who'd talked so lovingly about her little brother. Her heart sank even further when she realized that Jenn's surprise about Poppop being her brother and realizing that she was Micah's great-aunt was a lie.

The longer she stared, the more the Jenn she'd known started to feel like a dream. This Jenn, her *aunt* Jenn, felt more like the dark itself than another kid. Old and unknowable and terrifying.

"Why?" Micah asked.

"Why'd I take the bracelet?" Aunt Jenn stepped closer as if to touch it. Micah shied away from her, clutching it tighter. "It used to be my mom's. It *should* have been mine. It would have if I hadn't . . ." She shook her head. "I hadn't seen it in a long time. Since before I came here. I just wanted to hold it, at first."

She laughed. It wasn't a happy sound. "Then I realized that if you had it, Elijah must have given it to you. I don't know why he thought you deserved it; you couldn't even be bothered to keep it safe." The look she gave Micah was almost pitying. "You can't even keep a simple promise."

Micah flinched. "Where's Poppop?"

Aunt Jenn's frown disappeared, brightening into a wide smile. "Elijah? He's here. I'll take you to him. But we have so much to talk about first! We—"

"I want to see him."

She blinked. "I was talking."

"You can talk and bring him to me at the same time, can't you? If you can do everything else, that should be easy." She was still reeling from everything her great-aunt had admitted to in the last minute and a half, but her focus was still on Poppop. If Aunt Jenn had him, she could bring him to her, like she'd said. Once she was sure he was safe, they could leave. Somehow.

Micah didn't notice the dark shadows that flickered across her great-aunt's face. "If I bring him, will you listen to me?"

"Fine."

The word had barely left her lips before Poppop appeared.

And he'd barely solidified before she ran to wrap him in a hug . . . and kept running as she passed through him in a rush of mist and cold, almost straight into the wall behind him.

Micah steadied herself before she could crash head-first into it. She whirled around. "What did you do to him?"

"Nothing! He's just . . . adjusting." Aunt Jenn bit her lip. "I've never brought over an adult before."

Micah scowled. He didn't look fine. He was paler than she'd ever seen him, brown skin nearly gray. His eyes were open, but he stared blindly ahead as though he couldn't actually see anything.

116

"Poppop?" she whispered. If he answered, she could relax. She would know, at least, that he could *hear* her. "Are you okay?"

He didn't answer.

Aunt Jenn looked at her. "Now will you let me talk?"

"Why isn't *he* talking?"

"I told you—"

"Can he even see me?" She gripped the bracelet in her hand tighter. "Is he even—"

"He's fine!"

A light bulb overhead blew out. Everyone but Poppop jumped. Aunt Jenn ran a hand over her face.

"Sorry. I'm sorry. I just . . . This is a good thing. You'll see." She smiled slightly. "It's a little scary now. I get that. But I'm not alone. I mean, *we're* not alone." She looked at Micah. "You felt how hard that was. Being alone here."

Micah had. She might even have felt bad for Aunt Jenn if she weren't so focused on Poppop, who had barely blinked since he'd been there. So, she didn't answer. But her great-aunt didn't wait for her to speak. Instead, she kept talking. "I've been alone here for a long time. That's what happens when no one comes back for you. So I've had nothing to do but remember. It's the only thing I really could do here, at first."

"At first?"

Micah inched closer to Poppop, shivering at the cold that surrounded him. She could feel it on her own skin the closer she got, tiny specks of ice that crept their way up her fingertips. She fought back a shiver and the sleepiness the cold brought with it. If she could just keep Aunt Jenn talking, she knew she could think of some way to get back.

"At first," Aunt Jenn agreed. "All the other stuff came later." She started pacing, and the lights flickered to life with her steps.

"We're in the basement," Theo whispered suddenly.

Micah blinked at the sound of his voice. He'd been so silent she'd almost forgotten he was there. The basement was a place she hadn't been to yet in any version of Finch House. There wasn't much of it to see. A concrete floor and concrete walls with pipes crisscrossing the ceiling. A long wooden workbench in the middle of the room and a single window across the entire far wall.

Aunt Jenn turned to Theo with a smile, ignoring the way he avoided her eyes. "We are. I used to hate it down here, but it's my favorite place now. I was still down here when Finch House really started to feel like mine."

"It's not yours," he pointed out. "It's mine."

He'd said almost the same thing to Micah by the attic door. He'd tried so hard to keep her from going in. And look what she'd done: gotten him stuck right along with her.

She shook her head, trying to ignore her guilt, and focused on Poppop. He was so quiet, so still. It was like he wasn't even there. Micah wasn't totally convinced that he was. She tried to take his hand, to thread their fingers together like doing so would bring whatever part of him that was missing back. But all she found was air. She balled her hand into a fist at her side instead.

"We'll be okay," she promised as quietly as she could.

It wasn't quiet enough. Her great-aunt rolled her eyes. It was still too easy to only see her as another kid. Just a twelve-year-old with eyes like creation. "I told you, he's fine. I'm making sure he is." Annoyance deepened into something darker. "That's more than he did for me."

"What do you mean?"

"I mean that he's done more for you in a couple of days than he has for me in . . . I don't really know how long. You want a colorful piece of trash sitting out on the sidewalk, and he comes to get it for you. I get stuck here, and what do I get? Nothing! Not any help, not even an apology."

119

Aunt Jenn took a deep breath. "Sorry. Everything is weird right now, but it'll get better fast. You'll both get used to being here, and I'll get used to having you around." She offered up a slight smile. "You won't have to be scared of anything."

Except you, Micah thought. She wasn't blind to her great-aunt's new moods, the way she could go so quickly from anger to happiness. She wasn't sure if it was an act or if it was genuine. She didn't know which was scarier.

"I have to go home," she said. "We"—she gestured to herself and Poppop and Theo—"all have to go. My mom will be worried, and Theo's sister will be worried and—"

"So? They might worry. But then they'll forget. They'll forget their worry and they'll forget you." Aunt Jenn reached for her hand, and Micah was too stunned to stop her. "Aren't you curious about what it's like to stay here?"

That was the problem. She was. She wanted to know how it felt to run through the halls without being afraid of the dark and to see inside the turret's circular room and explore the rest of the house's weird, hidden doors. She wanted to slip between the different versions of the house like a bug slipping through a crack in the wall, finding her own paths, exploring every new and old part of itself that Finch House had to offer.

But it wasn't just her. She'd gotten Theo stuck too. And her mom was waiting for her. And something was wrong with Poppop. Plus, she had school and her bike, even her new house. She had a *life*. Outside of Finch House. Far away from it. As curious as she was, there was a *whole world* to be curious about too.

Micah met Aunt Jenn's eyes. Dark met dark. "I don't want to stay," she said softly. "I want to go home."

Aunt Jenn snatched her hand away. She backed up, trembling now, and the floor and the walls and the ceiling all trembled with her. Rumbling with age, bricks ground against one another, and pipes groaned.

"You think that wasn't what I wanted too? To go home? You think I wanted to be alone?" She spread her arms wide, and the house reacted. The tool bench flew across the room. The window shattered.

"You think I wanted to be stuck here?"

"Micah," Theo whispered. He was suddenly much closer to her, clutching her wrist with both hands. "Micah, we should go."

Of course they should. But go where? And how? She looked at Poppop. Whatever was wrong with him, there was no way he'd be able to follow them.

"We can't," she whispered back. It was getting harder

to hear, harder to breathe, even, like Aunt Jenn was sucking all the air and warmth from the room. "I won't leave him."

As quickly as it started, everything stopped.

The basement went silent.

Aunt Jenn stood in the middle of the floor, broken glass at her feet, plaits unraveling, chest heaving.

"You should," she whispered. Her voice was hoarse. "You should leave him. He deserves a taste of his own medicine."

Micah was confused. Again. "What are you talking about?"

She ignored her. "It was easy to bring everyone else here. A little tug, some whispers, and they were still in their beds but just in my version of Finch House. But Elijah . . ." She scowled. "All this time and he *still* wouldn't come with me. He *still* wanted to run."

Micah's mind raced. She was trying her best to think of a plan, but Aunt Jenn was sucking her in. Making her curious. She wanted to know more almost as badly as she wanted to leave. She ignored Theo's wide, pleading eyes and the guilt she felt every time she met them. Here was her chance to find out everything Poppop was keeping from her and Mom.

Aunt Jenn laughed. It was full of anger. "All I've wanted this whole time was to see him again, and he never came. And when he finally does, when I can barely recognize him, he's just here for some stupid old chest! For you!" She smiled widely, like she'd won a prize. "But he got just close enough. I'd thank you for that, but you don't really deserve it."

Out of the corner of her eye, Micah saw Theo creeping toward the stairs. He was close and getting closer. He gestured frantically when their eyes met, but she shifted hers back to her great-aunt.

"Close enough for what?"

She knew the answer. But she didn't know if she was stalling to help Theo or just trying to put together the pieces of a puzzle Aunt Jenn had spread out for her.

Couldn't it be both?

"To bring him inside, of course."

"Why?" That was the most important question. "Just because you missed him? Because you thought he could help you leave? Because—"

"Because he's mine!" Aunt Jenn exclaimed. "He's *my* brother. He should have been here with me, not with you! You shouldn't have had him!"

Micah frowned. "I didn't make that decision."

"That doesn't make it any better. But that's not the only reason. I wanted out of my deal."

"What deal? With who?" She tried to think of who her great-aunt could have even made a deal with. There were only the other kids. Them and . . . "Finch House?"

One girl nodded. The other frowned. "But what does that mean? What did that have to do with anything? With taking Poppop?"

Aunt Jenn grinned. She looked like Micah had asked the very question she'd been waiting to answer. "I'll show you."

Her voice came from everywhere and nowhere at once, and the storm she'd raged earlier came roaring back. The cold shot up to blizzard levels. Everything groaned. And even though she'd had her eyes open the entire time, Micah looked around and found herself both completely alone and no longer in the basement at all.

chapter thirteen

S he was outside.

That was the first thing Micah noticed. She was outside, but there was no snow on the ground and no chill in her bones. Everything else came to her in pieces. The dim glow of streetlights. The old cars parked everywhere. And Finch House, back to its fading glory, broken down and overgrown again.

"What?" she whispered.

A voice in the dark shushed her, and Micah nearly screamed. She whirled around to face her shusher and froze.

A photograph stared back at her. At least, he looked like he'd stepped out of one. Because she recognized the boy gesturing for her to crouch behind a nearby bush with him. She'd just looked through a photo album full of pictures of him. And she had just seen him, or some version of him, frozen and ghostly in the basement.

"Poppop?"

He can't hear you. Aunt Jenn's voice buzzed in her head, flitting from one ear to the other. *This already happened.*

Micah dug her nails into her arm. "I don't understand."

If this was like her arrival in Finch House all over again, she couldn't do it. She couldn't be brave twice. She'd barely been brave the first time. In fact, all she'd been was lucky. If Aunt Jenn hadn't found her sitting in the hall, she'd probably still be there, praying the dark would leave her alone. It didn't even matter that she'd been the one to lure her there in the first place.

Pay attention, Aunt Jenn scolded her. *You wanted to know what I meant, then pay attention.*

As if her whispered word was law, Micah found herself moving forward. She followed Poppop—*"Elijah,"* Aunt Jenn corrected in a whisper—around a rotting wood fence and up to a dusty window. He cupped his hands around his eyes to peek inside, and she did the same.

So, this was Finch House as Poppop had seen it.

She squinted.

Inside was a mess of broken and covered furniture and the silhouette of the house's grand staircase. She caught a glimpse of a huge chandelier winking with the light of the moon pouring in from outside when she looked up.

"It's amazing," Elijah whispered next to her. His reaction now was so far from the reaction he would have in the future, when he refused to even get close to the house or let her near it. "Let's find a way in."

"Let's *not*." Micah glanced around anxiously. Tipton Street was so quiet at night, and she had the feeling that they really, really weren't supposed to be there.

We weren't. Not here, not even in this part of town. But our dad told us about this place, and we wanted to see it for ourselves. Weren't any houses with towers where we lived, and here was a perfectly good one nobody even lived in.

"You're right," Elijah said, but he was responding to whatever Aunt Jenn had said then, unheard by her, and not what Aunt Jenn had said now. "We'll try the back door."

So, they crept to the back. Weeds as high as her knee brushed against Micah. She stared hard at the ground to avoid stepping on twigs or leaves or anything that might echo loudly on the too-quiet street.

And they were close. So close. Close enough that she could reach out and grab that back doorknob, and all she had to do was *twist*—

Here they come.

"Hey! What are you two doing here?"

There was one voice and then more, one question and then more. Before she or Elijah got a chance to answer, people were chasing them, and then they were running.

As fast as they could. As hard as they could.

Elijah's hand was in hers until it wasn't. Her heart raced faster, and Micah couldn't distinguish her own thoughts from Aunt Jenn's voice looping in her head.

I lost him. I lost him. I lost him.

It had always been dark, but panic made everything darker. Micah stumbled through Finch House's overgrown backyard, fear urging her to call out for Elijah and fear keeping her from doing it. Footsteps and voices still followed her, too close and too loud.

"Get back here, girl!" a man yelled.

Just a little longer, Aunt Jenn urged.

So, Micah kept running. As quickly as her legs would take her in the dark through an unfamiliar yard. And there was the fence again, closer, closer. All she had to do was find Elijah, and then they could climb it, run back to the front, and grab their bikes. They'd go home and—

There!

Somehow, she recognized the way Elijah ran even in the dark. That quick stride of his legs, the way the air almost seemed to get out of his way.

"Elijah!" she whispered as loud as she dared.

He didn't hear her. Or maybe he didn't care. He kept running, and she kept following him, and then she was

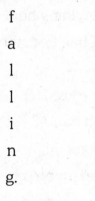

f
a
l
l
i
n
g.

chapter fourteen

Micah was lying on her back, staring up at the hole her body had created.

Everything hurt.

Every inch of her, from the curls brushing her neck to her pinkie toe.

She shut her eyes. Her head throbbed, but the floor was cool beneath her. All she wanted was to go to sleep.

"You have to get up."

Micah cracked an eye open. Aunt Jenn wasn't just in her head anymore. Instead, she stood above her, looking down with a mix of sympathy, apology, and determination that only made Micah's head hurt more.

She groaned. "No."

Even as she said it, her body jerked her up into a sitting position.

"Now you're going to crawl back over to the cellar

doors—that's what you fell through, by the way—and try to climb out."

And she did.

She fought it. She tried to lock her limbs in place. She ground her teeth together. But her body still walked toward the cellar doors.

"Why?" she asked. She was still in too much pain to ask a proper question. "How?"

"I told you—this has happened before." Aunt Jenn nodded toward the rotted, cracked doors. The hole wasn't Micah-shaped, just wide and dangerous-looking. "Climb through."

She didn't have a choice. She climbed up toward the hole and its jagged, wooden edges and was halfway out.

And then she just . . . glitched.

She was back on the ground, staring at the hole.

"Again," Aunt Jenn said. And Micah's body obeyed.

Again and again and again.

Over and over until she thought she might lose her mind from both the pain and the lack of control. She couldn't even scream how she wanted. She was too tired.

"Okay," Micah whispered. She was on her back again. The floor was still cool, and everything still hurt. "Okay, I get it."

She didn't know how much time had passed or how many times she'd crawled over to the doors and been reset. She just knew that she was alone. That the voices and footsteps had all gone away, and none of them had come back for her.

Finally, Aunt Jenn sighed, sitting cross-legged beside her. Micah felt something in her body loosen. She clenched and unclenched her hands. She wriggled her toes inside her shoes. Her body was hers again.

"No, you don't. I went easy on you. I must have tried to leave this place a hundred times. And every time, the same thing happened." She traced a finger through the dirt on the floor. First a *J*, then an *R*. Her initials.

"Eventually, I tried going the other way. *Into* the house. That worked."

Micah nodded, but she was still stuck on how Elijah—Poppop—had run away. Run and hadn't come back in all the time she tried to get out.

Run and left her behind.

"Maybe he was going to get help."

She hadn't realized she'd said it out loud until Aunt Jenn snorted. "I told you, I went easy on you. I was here for . . . so long. No one came. Not the police. Not help. And *not* Elijah."

The image of his back to her flickered to life in Micah's mind. She pushed it down. "Poppop wouldn't do that."

She expected an argument, but her great-aunt only shrugged. "I don't know your poppop," she said. "I only know Elijah."

Micah shook her head, trying not to think of all the different people one person could be, trying to remember their earlier conversation. "But when you did make a deal? What was it?"

Her great-aunt was silent, and, in the silence, Micah kept her ears open. Whether it was for the angry voices of the men that had chased them or for Theo's voice, another world away, trying to reach her, she wasn't sure. But too much quiet made her nervous—like it was building up to an explosion of noise.

No explosion came.

Eventually, Aunt Jenn said, "Finch House felt bad for me, I think. That's the only reason I can come up with. That, and it was lonely and maybe it felt how lonely I was, too."

She scowled and swiped at the ground, erasing any trace of her initials.

"It didn't happen right away. It was just me in a house, at first. Alone . . . but not lonely. It felt like someone was with me everywhere I went, like having an imaginary friend all over again. But . . ."

"But?"

"But it wasn't my house. My parents weren't there. Elijah wasn't there. And I couldn't leave. If I got too close to the front door or a window, everything changed. If I tried one of the phones, they just beeped in my ear. But I found a door I'd never seen one day. It was wide open, so I walked in. That's when I made the deal. If I stayed, I would have control. I could do whatever I wanted, control whatever I liked, learn all the secrets I knew the house had."

She sighed. "I couldn't leave anyway. It seemed like an easy choice. But I didn't want to be alone anymore. I said that."

Micah leaned in, caught up in the story. "What did the house say?"

Aunt Jenn lifted her head. "It said I didn't have to be. It said we'd work together, like a body and its Heart, and we'd never have to be alone.

"But that was a lie." She scoffed. "All the kids I brought here were scared of me. Not the house—me. Finch House 'saved' them like it had saved me. No deals, but it gave them rooms with doors I couldn't walk through and places they could hide away, to never have to talk to me. It made friends with them by making me the monster that wandered the halls."

Micah tried to imagine how lonely that might be: becoming a monster by accident. "But you still brought them here. You still took them from their families until they were just as stuck as you."

Aunt Jenn scowled, rubbing her eyes with a sleeve. "No one is as stuck as me," she said. A moment passed, and her scowl softened. "But yeah, I did. Of course I did. People started living here, with their parents and siblings and pets, and I just—I'd just get so mad. So jealous. So sometimes I brought them here on purpose. But other times I'd try not to. I'd try not to even *think* about it, but the next thing I knew, they were here anyway. I never knew if it was me or Finch House that did it."

If Aunt Jenn and Finch House both took people, were both types of monsters, then where was the line between them that said this one is a girl and this one is a house?

Did Aunt Jenn even know herself?

She shrugged. "I figured if I did it enough, people would stop moving here. They'd give up. No one else would get stuck. That was true, for a while."

But Theo had moved there.

And Micah had broken a promise and gone inside.

And Poppop had gotten too close.

"How'd you think me and Poppop would break the deal?"

"I didn't. I mean, not at first. I'd offered Finch House the other kids I took before. I suggested we switch places, and I'd be like anyone else in the house, not controlling anything, not taking anyone. Maybe then I could make friends. Maybe I would finally stop feeling so alone. But it always refused. None of those kids had come there willingly, it said."

"Neither did Poppop," Micah pointed out. She thought of him coming to get the chest for her. "Not inside, anyway."

"I took Elijah because I wanted him. He left me and I was so angry, but . . . I never stopped missing him."

Micah asked, "And me?"

But she knew the answer.

Aunt Jenn had taken her bracelet.

She'd taken Poppop.

Micah, though, had willingly gone in search of both.

Aunt Jenn looked at her. She looked like a kid again. Like the girl who'd become her friend in the hallway of a house that gobbled kids up.

Unless Micah looked too hard.

Then her eyes looked just like the windows of a house where no one lived. Where all the lights were out and no one would come to the door if you rang the bell.

"You," she said. "You had everything that should have been mine." Aunt Jenn's smile was not a smile at all. "It only made sense that you should be the Heart too."

chapter fifteen

I f you think about it," she continued, "it makes sense. You had Elijah." She stuck out her thumb. "My mom's bracelet." She added a finger. "A family." Another finger. "A life where you could come and go and do what you wanted. You had everything."

Aunt Jenn's fingers curled back into her palm to form a fist at her side. "So, I thought, why shouldn't I bring you here to see how it feels when all that's ripped away? You got one of the best parts of my life. I needed to make sure you got the bad, too.

"But it's not all bad if you think about it. Not really. If you're in charge, this place doesn't have to change. Nothing does. I know you're moving; I heard you and Theo talking about it."

She smiled, too wide with too many teeth. Micah wasn't sure if it was meant to be sincere or taunting. "But if you're the Heart, then there would be no more move—no new house, no new school or new friends. Everything could stay the same. It could change as little or as much as you want it to. You could even bring your mom here."

Micah tried not to give in to the awful feeling that was spreading through her like poison. No, she'd keep asking questions. Questions were how you got answers. Answers were how you made plans.

"What makes you think Finch House would even accept me?"

"You came here willingly," Aunt Jenn said like it was obvious. She paused, then added, "And we're related! Whatever magic or energy the house uses, maybe our connection will make it easier to switch from me to you."

That reminded Micah of school, how sometimes her teachers called her Aniyah, the name of the other curly-haired Black girl in her class, even though they had nothing in common. No actual connection.

"What if it doesn't?"

"It will. Here's the thing," Aunt Jenn said, standing suddenly. She stretched, long and catlike, until something cracked. "If you agree to become the new Heart of the House, I'll let all the other kids go."

The basement faded. Or it changed. Or it had always

been the way it was. Whatever had happened, Poppop and Theo were there again. Theo staring wide-eyed at her by the stairs, Poppop still staring at nothing.

"You could let them go without me."

Aunt Jenn tilted her head as she stared at her. "I could. But what good would that do for me?"

Micah stood slowly. The broken glass from earlier, the glass that hadn't been there a second ago, crunched underfoot. She understood something.

Nothing about her great-aunt was real.

Her story, maybe, but not her tears. Not her sadness. Not even what had sounded a little bit like regret. If she felt those things, that was before. Back when she was just a girl and not a girl with a haunted house's power.

"I thought you felt bad about bringing them here. I thought you wanted to help them."

"I want to help *me*. And that can help them, too, if you agree. If you don't, you're just leaving them here. Stuck in Finch House. Forever."

"I thought you wanted to be my friend," Micah said before she could stop herself.

Something dark and complicated flickered across her great-aunt's face. "Yeah, well, friends help friends. All I'm asking you to do is help me."

Micah glared, ignoring the tears starting to blur her vision. "You're not asking. You're trying to guilt me." Sacrificing her, even. She tried not to focus on how much that hurt.

Aunt Jenn shrugged. "I'm bargaining."

Micah took a deep breath. She drew on all the courage in her belly. "Then the answer's no."

Her great-aunt blinked. "No?"

"No," Micah repeated. She kept her hands at her sides, squeezing them together as guilt hit her. "Like you said, they're already stuck. What difference does that make?"

Out of the corner of her eye, she could see Theo's horrified face. She hoped none of the other kids were listening.

Sorry, she apologized silently. *Sorry, sorry.*

Getting herself, Theo, and Poppop out was the most important thing. If she was free, she could figure out how to help everyone else out later.

But she needed to be free first.

She needed to go home.

For a moment, Aunt Jenn looked thoughtful. And then she sighed, walking over to Theo without a word. He was taller than her by a few inches, but she simply stood on her tiptoes to throw an arm casually around his shoulder. It looked awkward with the height difference. Theo looked too terrified to move.

"You really don't care about the other kids?"

"No," Micah lied.

"But you care about this one. You care about Elijah. So, we're going to make our own deal, okay? You agree to become the Heart of the House, and you can help everyone. You can let them all go. But." Her voice sharpened, and her eyes met Micah's. It was like staring down into the stairwell again. "If you say no, Elijah and Theo stay here with me."

Micah squeezed her hands together even tighter to stop herself from trembling. She was pretty sure it didn't work. "And what about me?"

Aunt Jenn's smile was just a flash of teeth. "We're friends. I'll let you go. But you wouldn't be able to come back."

She could leave, then.

Leave but never get the chance to see Theo or Pop-pop again.

Before Micah could say anything—yes or no, stop or please or wait—her great-aunt's arm tightened around Theo. And Theo's body reacted immediately.

He gasped, once, softly. And then he started fading in bits and pieces. His eyes glazed over. His pale skin paled even further, until he looked like he'd been sitting out in the cold for too long. And he lost . . . something. Whatever it was that made a person look solid and alive.

Aunt Jenn had put her arm around him and sucked the life straight out.

"You don't get to be free *and* keep everyone you care about, Micah. That's not how bargaining works."

Micah's mind went blank. When it started up again, she barely noticed how hard she was shaking. All she could see were Poppop and Theo and the new emptiness in both of them. All she could think was that this was her fault. If she hadn't come inside . . . if she hadn't been such a baby about wanting the chest . . . if she'd just ridden her bike straight past Finch House and gone home . . .

Her chest tightened. She took breath after breath but got less air each time.

Focus, Micah, she told herself.

She could fix this. She could! All she had to do was agree to become the Heart of Finch House.

Agree, and stay there forever.

Agree, and never see Mom or Poppop again.

Agree, and . . .

There was so much after "and."

"I don't want to rush you," she barely heard Aunt Jenn say, "but the clock's ticking. The longer you stay here, the harder it will be to leave, even if I want you to go."

Quietly, soft as a heartbeat, a ticking began deep inside Finch House.

Tick, tick, tick.

"You can call for me when you decide. Or whisper it. Whichever. I'll hear you either way."

The girl who was not a girl moved her arm from around Theo's shoulders to wave at her.

When Micah blinked, the three of them were gone.

Micah had no idea what she was doing or what she was going to do. When she had a choice, it was usually easy to make. This ice cream or that one. Pizza or chicken tenders for lunch. Taking out the trash or doing the dishes.

This choice was not easy. It was impossible. Worse, it didn't even involve only her. Breaking her promise had gotten Poppop into this mess, and her stubbornness had dragged Theo into it too. Now they were relying on her to fix it. To *help* them.

But helping meant sacrificing the rest of her life. Not just all the people and things she knew now, but everything and everyone she might have known when she grew up.

That seemed much scarier somehow—giving up things she couldn't even imagine having in the first place.

Micah walked upstairs and over to the first window she saw. When she looked through it, though, all she could see was herself, her eyes wide and frightened, her bottom lip trapped between her teeth. Even when she tried to squint past her reflection, there was nothing. Tipton Street, a street she knew pretty well, was just a blur. There were no houses and no street and no snow.

It was like nowhere else even existed.

She yanked herself away, trying her best to ignore the tears stinging her eyes.

She'd already cried in this house once, and she didn't have time to do it again. The *tick, tick, tick* echoed in her ears if she stood still for too long.

"You're okay," she reassured herself, taking a few deep breaths. "Everything will be okay."

For that to be true, though, she couldn't just stand there feeling sorry for herself. No matter how badly she wanted to. No, she needed to find Finch House.

Whatever or whoever it was. If the house had made a deal with Aunt Jenn, then someone had to have offered it. For all the weirdness that she'd seen in the house so far, talking walls wasn't one of them.

So, she did what she did best: she explored.

She ran all the way up to the attic and all the way back down to the basement.

She didn't let herself think:

- about how empty Poppop and Theo had looked
- about how sick of this house she was getting

She only looked:

- in the crawl space
- in every room whose doors would open for her
- deep into herself for the courage Nana had
  promised was always there

She found new things—a tiny fountain at the end of a hall shaped like a blooming flower. A painting of a fat little pig wearing a diamond crown. A library with a door twice her size full of only books whose covers looked like fairy tales—but none of them were useful. None of them told her where to find Finch House.

She talked to the house as she searched. "I know you can hear me," she said. "And I know that you know I'm looking for you. Directions would be nice! Or even a sign that I'm on the right track," she muttered. Considering she'd passed the same row of paintings and pictures twice now, she wasn't too confident.

"I just want to make a deal."

She paused midstep. She was pretty sure she'd seen most of Finch House by now—Aunt Jenn's tour had been pretty thorough, after all, and she'd wandered for a long time on her own before she'd been found by her. But the part of Finch House that always drew her to it, stealing her attention whenever she biked past, was one the house hadn't shown her. One that Aunt Jenn had refused to take her to, even.

Trust me, she'd said. *There's nothing for you up there.*

But Micah didn't trust her anymore. And if her great-aunt hadn't wanted her to see the turret, that was all the more reason for Micah to find her way up there.

Maybe that was the key, wanting to find it for a reason, not just because she was curious. Or maybe she'd just missed it before. Either way, when Micah turned the corner, there was a staircase.

It was almost identical to the house's main staircase except that it was a spiral. A perfect spiral like one of her curls just after she washed her hair—it curved in on itself and went up, up, up.

Micah went up too.

She didn't know what she'd expected when she got to the top, but it wasn't a door with an eye for a peephole.

She stared at the door.

It stared back.

Micah tried the handle. It was locked.

She tried again. And again, and again. And every time she tried and it didn't work, she felt her frustration grow.

"Please," she whispered as she rattled the doorknob for the hundredth time. "Please, please let me in."

Asking nicely didn't work.

Neither did banging loudly on the door until her hand throbbed and her head ached along with it. "C'mon," she urged. "Let me in!" She swore she could hear the *tick, tick, tick*ing through the floorboards. Feel time running out in her bones. She knocked against the thick wood with her feet, kicking repeatedly. "Unless you want to be stuck with Aunt Jenn forever, make this easier for both of us and open." Kick. "The." Kick. "Door."

She paused, but the door still didn't open. Finch House didn't answer her.

Micah groaned. She stuffed both hands in her pockets and glared at the stairs, wondering what new part of the house would be waiting for her when she reached the bottom.

Her left hand wrapped around something cold, and she quickly yanked it out with a gasp.

She counted to five and unclenched her fist.

In the middle of her palm was a key. The key she'd taken from Renee's shoebox on a whim. The key she'd forgotten all about.

But there was no way, right? Out of all the doors in Finch House, seen and unseen, this door couldn't be the one it unlocked.

. . . Could it?

The small bird perched on the length of it stared up at her like it dared her to try.

Micah took a few deep breaths. She'd try it. At this point, she wasn't sure she had much to lose.

She stuck the key into the lock and turned. The peephole eye slowly slid sideways to look at her.

At the same time that she gasped, she heard a click.

She tried the knob. It was as cold in her hand as the key had been, almost cold enough to hurt.

It turned.

The door opened.

Before she could chicken out, Micah stepped into the turret room.

Slowly, like it was giving her time to back out or run back downstairs, the door shut behind her.

chapter sixteen

The room was full of windows and full of winter sunlight.

Micah shielded her eyes. After dark hallways and darker basements, she'd almost forgotten what sunlight was. Clearly the turret room hadn't. There were at least five windows along the curved wall in front of her, light pouring through them and their flowy white curtains like honey.

She wanted to be a cat very much at that moment. To curl up in a patch of sunlight and forget about everything and everyone else. But that wasn't what she was there for.

She was there to make a deal.

In front of the windows, in the middle of the room, was an easel with a blank canvas. And in front of the easel, a woman formed.

Not appeared. *Formed.*

She pulled herself together from shadows and sunlight until she was a hazy outline. Then, despite a lack of paint or brushes, she began to paint.

At least, Micah assumed it was her. Paint appeared on the canvas—a stroke of red here, a swirl of yellow there—too abstract for her to make out what it was going to be, if anything.

She opened her mouth to speak.

The shadow-and-sunlight woman beat her to it.

"Michaela," she said. Her voice was all warmth. "We've been waiting for you."

Did she mean "we" like there were other shadow-and-sunlight people? Or "we" like her and Finch House? Or "we" like—

The woman turned to look at her with a smile. She didn't quite have a face like the other people Micah had met in Finch House. Or like a person at all, really. Just an outline of one—an impression.

"Relax," she said. "I can hear your thoughts racing from here. And no," she added before Micah's thoughts could race any faster, "I can't actually hear them. More like . . . feel them, you could say. But I will answer any questions you have if I can. There must be many."

Oh, there were. But Micah's brain was still busy trying to process just what the woman—human or ghost or shadow—was.

So, she only stared for a while, and the shadow-and-sunlight woman painted. She hummed as she did, softly enough to be the wind, a song that Micah had never heard before but that made her feel a bit like a baby being lulled to sleep. Along with the sunlight, the music helped her relax.

"I want to make a deal," she said finally.

The painting stopped. It was a riot of colors now with no real image. Just paint swirled in all different directions. She thought it was pretty.

"I know."

"Then if you know, you know why."

"I do."

"So?" Micah asked.

"So?" the woman repeated.

"So, yes or no?"

She tilted her head, and the shadows rearranged themselves. Micah got a glimpse of bright yellow eyes and a soft smile before the shadows settled again. "You haven't actually asked us anything. You must speak up for what you want."

Micah sighed. Apparently, this wasn't going to be as straightforward as she thought.

"Are you Finch House?" she asked.

"You may think of me as the house if you like. I was formed from it, and we are hard to separate in any way that means something." She paused. "Like the core of an apple or a pit in a cherry."

"You can take both of those out," Micah pointed out.

"You could," Finch House agreed. "But by the time you reach it, the fruit is usually no longer whole."

"So, what? Without you, Finch House doesn't exist?"

"The part that would make it Finch House and not, say, your house, yes."

Micah was quiet in her thoughtfulness. "Okay," she said finally. "But why are you here? You said you were formed—who formed you?"

"I don't know. I'm not sure that it is even very important. I protect the people inside the house. When there is no one to protect, I protect the house itself." Micah caught the briefest frown as sunlight flashed within the shadows like lightning. "It was stolen once. Stolen and left empty for a long time. It is an unfortunate thing, the absence of people in a space that should be abundant." The room filled with noise as she spoke. Sounds that

Micah was familiar with, like the stacking of dishes or sports on the TV, people laughing and talking, and others that she wasn't, like the sour notes of a horn being played.

It all stopped abruptly.

"Is that why you let Aunt Jenn take all those kids? To fill up the space?"

She could feel her curiosity and confusion shaping into anger. Micah didn't see how that was fair, to take other people from their lives to make up for the emptiness of your own. Or, in this case, the emptiness of a house.

"They were all living here, at least some of them, so you wouldn't have been empty. You wouldn't need to fill space."

"We are a house," Finch House said simply. "We do not control what the people who live here, or visit, do. We only protect them."

Micah shook her head. "You're lying. You do control it. You made Aunt Jenn your Heart. *You* did that. *You* trapped her here, and *you* let her trap other people. *I'm a house* is not an excuse."

The house frowned. "We protected them as best we saw fit. We gave them rooms, places for privacy." Micah

155

opened her mouth to argue, but the house kept talking. "We helped you in the same way, allowing you moments of freedom. We pulled you away from her. You could have chosen to leave, but you didn't. We don't believe in taking away choices. Jennifer wanted to bring people here, to the part of the house where she exists, to keep her company. That was her choice, and we supported her."

Micah tried not to think about how close an eye Finch House must have kept on her to let her move between the different versions of it so seamlessly. "But you could have let her go. She wouldn't have been lonely if she were allowed to leave."

Finch House hesitated. The woman *and* the house. The floors creaked with indecision. Even the steady stream of sunlight flickered. "We were protecting her."

"Why?"

The painting on the easel drew Micah's attention as it became something new. Gone were the various strokes of colors. Now it was almost photographic, an exact replica of a scene Micah had already seen: Aunt Jenn falling into Finch House's basement.

The colors were mostly muted. Grays and blacks for the floor and shadows. Dark brown for the crisscross beams of the ceiling. And then, as Micah watched, there was a new color.

A deep shade of red around her great-aunt.

Micah shook her head. She'd seen what had happened. She'd experienced it for herself. Aunt Jenn had gotten up. She'd tried to leave, over and over again. She hadn't just lain there. She wasn't . . .

You're running out of time, she'd said.

Maybe she hadn't only been trying to scare Micah into taking her deal. Maybe she'd really meant it. Finch House was an in-between type of place; that much was clear. Maybe if a person stayed too long, there wasn't enough of them left to go anywhere else. Not on their own.

Micah swallowed her nerves and focused on the room. The bright sunlight had turned orange, as though the sun were setting, though it had only been a few minutes. "You don't have to protect anyone, though. You can let them all go. Be a normal house. People live here now, so you won't be lonely. And even if they move, they fixed you up enough that people will keep coming."

It was simple, she thought. Pretty house + new family = no loneliness. No loneliness = a normal Finch House. A normal Finch House didn't need to keep kids in its walls. It didn't need a keeper at all.

Apparently, Finch House didn't agree. Shadows swirled around her faster, the sunlight getting lost in her depths, and she grew until she was a column of shapeless shadow nearly touching the ceiling. Bright yellow eyes glared down at Micah. She resisted the urge to wilt beneath them.

"We were not fixed!" Finch House roared. "We were ruined! So much history, so much charm, lost, and for what? Stainless steel? Open concepts? If they wanted a different house, then they should have bought one!"

"Sure, they made changes. And maybe you didn't like them." Micah thought of how run-down it had looked before. The cracks and leaks and holes everywhere. The rotting front porch. "But change isn't always bad. Not if it helps you."

Finch House shrank a little. Not enough to be human-size, but enough that it didn't look quite so scary. "We were helping ourselves."

"By kidnapping kids. All you did was make yourself a haunted house."

"We were protecting ourselves. Few people go near the things that frighten them."

"Maybe," Micah said. "But you don't have to get that close to a house to tear it down. What would you watch over then? Would you even exist?"

Before Finch House could respond, Micah shook her head. She'd questioned and argued long enough. It was now or never, and she didn't see any other way forward for any of them but to do this now.

"Make me the Heart of Finch House."

Silently, Finch House shrank back down to its original size. Wide yellow eyes like an owl's blinked at Micah. "We have a Heart."

"Yeah, and she hates it. She doesn't want to do it anymore."

"She agreed to it."

"A long time ago!" She took a deep breath. "Can't you just undo it?"

"Jennifer is the first person we brought here, and we did so for her own good. What we've given her can't simply be taken back. It connects us. It was a . . . gift. Without her, our energy is limited. Without us, her energy is nonexistent."

Micah pressed both hands together like a prayer, but she didn't pray. She only dug into the thin bones of each hand with her fingertips, feeling her heartbeat in her palms. Her eyes drifted back toward the canvas in the middle of the room. All that red in the middle of so much black and gray.

159

She shut her eyes. "She can't just be one of the kids here, then? She's the Heart, or she's nothing?"

If Aunt Jenn stayed the Heart, Theo and Poppop were trapped.

If Micah became the Heart, who knew what would happen to her great-aunt.

She could save some people.

She couldn't save everyone.

Still, she had to try.

"Your deal with Aunt Jenn was new, right? The first one you'd ever made?" Finch House nodded. "And it's limited because of what happened to her. She *has* to stay here. But I wouldn't have to."

She nodded to herself and started walking from one end of the small, circular room to the other. Micah understood what it was to want to know things. How frustrating it could be not to have answers. And there was a whole world out there beyond the sidewalk of things that Finch House didn't, and might never, know.

"You want to protect the house, right? But you can't do that just being stuck in here. You don't even know what's happening down the street. But I do. I ride my bike all over. Mom drives me around. Whatever I know, you would too, wouldn't you? And I can go lots of places, see and hear and learn all kinds of things."

People could explore the things they were curious about. Houses couldn't.

But they did have their own things worth exploring.

"Make me the Heart, and I'll help you see the world." Or, at least, New Jersey. She bit her lip. "But you have to show me your world, too."

Whatever allowed Finch House to change shape and keep people and become giant columns of shadow, Micah wanted to be part of it. At the very least, she wanted to know how it all worked. How far it stretched and how deep it went.

If she knew how the things that scared her worked— if she could learn them like she'd learned how to read or do multiplication—there would be no reason to be afraid.

Finch House looked thoughtful.

Micah tried not to let her nerves show. Her heart beat too loudly. Her vision blurred.

She tried to study Finch House, but it was hard to study a shadow and even harder to do when she was on the verge of a panic attack.

This was her best bet, her only plan.

She really hoped it worked.

Finch House had started painting again, she realized as she waited for an answer. The earlier painting was gone. On the canvas now was a circular swirl of blue and white and green. Some version of the earth seen from far away.

"How big is the world, Michaela?" the house asked softly.

Science wasn't her strongest subject.

"I don't know," she said honestly. "Bigger than this house."

The shadow-and-sunlight woman hummed. Micah looked out the window to see the tail end of the sun slipping away, orange disappearing, deep blue creeping in.

The turret room filled with moonlight.

The *tick, tick, tick* of time was audible beneath the quiet.

chapter seventeen

W ell? Am I here because you made up your mind, or because you want to try to change mine?" Aunt Jenn asked. She leaned against the banister of the main-floor stairs, smirking slightly. "I'm open to either, really. It's your own time you'd be wasting."

Micah had called her almost immediately after she'd left the turret room, so she didn't give herself time to overthink. It hadn't helped. Her mind was racing anyway. Whatever happened now was it.

"I made up my mind," she said. She didn't pace. She tried her best to stay still, to stand by her decision.

"Well?"

Her great-aunt tried her best to look uninterested and failed. Her eyes were wide with expectation. She was nearly vibrating from the wait.

"I have a question first, though." Micah had many

questions, in fact. But this was the one she needed an answer to before she gave hers. "Have you been angry with Poppop for leaving you this whole time?"

Aunt Jenn blinked. Then she sighed. "In the beginning, yes. Definitely, yes. You saw how things were. There wasn't much to do except be angry at him. Especially when I saw him again, coming to get that chest. He was an adult! He got to grow up and have a life and a family, and that whole time I was stuck right here. Nothing had changed for me, not even how I looked. He'd gotten to do all that only because he left me behind. But in the middle?"

She shrugged. "I didn't forget. That was impossible. But I . . . didn't think about it so much. It was less about how I'd gotten here and more about *being* here. Learning how to use everything Finch House gave me and what to do with it. Trying to come up with new ways to leave without the house realizing it. So, no, I haven't been angry with him this whole time. Just when I remembered."

The sadness on her face shifted as Micah looked at her, fading into annoyance. Standing taller, she tossed a braid behind her shoulder. "Enough talking. Are you going to accept my deal or not?"

"I can't."

"What do you mean you can't?"

"I made my own deal."

Before she could explain or apologize, the house exploded.

At least, it seemed to.

The brightest light Micah had ever seen emerged from everywhere at once. The floorboards, the windows, even the paneling on the walls. It erupted from furniture and the frayed edges of a nearby rug and the worryingly shaky chandelier above them.

And it felt like it erupted from her, too, her brown skin glowing when she glanced down at herself until keeping her eyes open was too much.

The house shook and groaned. The floors rumbled enough that she nearly fell over. She wondered what would happen to everyone if Finch House collapsed in a heap around them.

Luckily, she didn't have to find out. With a final low groan, the house stopped and the light slowly faded.

Micah peeked one eye open.

Everything looked exactly the same except for two things.

1. Aunt Jenn was on her knees, staring at everything in confusion and looking very much like a normal twelve-year-old girl.
2. Micah's chest felt like it was on fire.

It wasn't a painful type of fire, or even the burning itch she got that warned her of an incoming panic attack. It was something warmer. Unfamiliar. Like someone had opened her up and stuck a mini sun in her rib cage. She checked the parts of herself that she could see, but nothing looked strange. She wasn't glowing anymore. She wasn't suddenly made of shadow-and-sunlight.

Whatever Finch House had done, however it had changed her, she didn't think it was visible.

"What did you do?" Jenn whispered. It was hard to think of her as anyone's aunt now that she looked like a kid again, lost and alone in a big house that she was no longer connected to.

"I don't know," Micah admitted. "I think I helped."

She hoped she had. She hoped she hadn't made everything worse.

As if her words unlocked something, kid-shaped shadows started to appear around them.

By the stairs and near the front door, in the hall and farther into the house, toward the kitchen. The shadows quickly faded to reveal person after person, their expressions all mirroring Jenn's. Shock. Confusion. Uncertainty. Micah expected them to solidify, to change in some way that meant that they were free now, but they didn't. They just stood and stared at both of them until a soft noise drew everyone's attention away.

Micah turned to look. With just the soft click of a lock and the low creak of hinges, Finch House's front door had opened.

It didn't lead anywhere. At least it didn't look like it did. Certainly not to the snowy yard and snowier street that Micah had left behind that morning. But it must have looked like something to the rest of them. There was a collective gasp, and then everyone started talking at once, whispers that grew louder and louder as the other kids formed groups and pairs and stole glances at the door.

Micah turned back to Jenn.

She was looking at the door too. She'd gotten quickly to her feet and took a few steps forward, only to pause. She stayed frozen for a few breaths. Then she turned her attention to Micah. Micah resisted the urge to flinch back

167

as Jenn walked toward her, but there wasn't much that was scary about her now. There was no obvious circle of power around her, nothing warm or magnetic that marked her as Important.

She was just a girl again.

A confused girl with tears in her eyes and a tremor in her hands. She didn't stop until she was standing in front of Micah, close enough to count her eyelashes.

"You made a deal with the house," she said. It wasn't a question.

Micah nodded. She wanted to ask Jenn if she was terrified, too, when she agreed. She wanted to know if she'd met the shadow-and-sunlight woman. But it seemed rude to ruin her plans and try to bond at the same moment, even if her great-aunt had been willing to serve her up to Finch House on a platter in exchange for her own freedom.

"Everyone's free to go," she said quietly, looking toward all the people still gathered nervously around the open door. "That means you, too."

She'd figured it out, at the end. Right before she made the deal. If she was the Heart, that meant she and Finch House were connected. Its energy was her energy. And just because she had it didn't mean she had to take away the energy that allowed her great-aunt to continue existing.

All she had to do was treat her like any other kid in the house.

It was strange. Micah could feel them all, like there were invisible strings connecting them to her. It reminded her of the time she'd seen a teacher walking with a group of toddlers, each of them holding on to the ring of one long leash as they crossed the street together, the teacher responsible for every one of them.

Jenn narrowed her eyes like she didn't believe her. Then she looked longingly back at the door. "How?"

"Does it matter?" It seemed like bragging to say that Micah had made the same deal Jenn had—she'd just had enough leverage to keep her freedom.

Jenn hesitated, eyes flickering between Micah and the door. "What about Elijah?"

"*Everyone* can go," she repeated. But her eyes flitted around the room. She'd expected Poppop and Theo to appear with everyone else, but she didn't see them. She tried not to think about whether a house could change its mind.

We did not. Both are here.

Micah froze. She turned in a slow, stiff circle, but no

one but Jenn was close enough to hear so clearly. "Did you hear that?"

Jenn tore her gaze from the door to look at her. She stared quietly, as if she were figuring something out, then shook her head. "Not anymore, no." Her lips curled into a slight smile. "You should get used to it."

Micah nodded slowly, trying not to focus on the weight of the voice in her head. If she focused, she could almost see the shadow-and-sunlight woman in her turret room, humming and painting as day turned to night over and over again outside her window.

Instead, she focused on looking for Poppop and Theo. It was surprisingly easy to do, considering they were walking over to her.

Without a word, she ran forward to wrap Poppop in a hug and relaxed fully when she could actually feel him—his arms warm and safe around her, his heart pounding away beneath her cheek.

"You're okay," she whispered, looking up at him. She could barely see through her tears, but she knew enough to know that he looked like himself again.

"I'm all right, Turtle." His voice was a quiet rasp. His lips were warm on her skin where he pressed them softly against her forehead.

"And you're not mad at me? For coming in here? For breaking my promise?"

He squeezed her tighter. "I couldn't be anything right now but happy to see you. Couldn't be much happier, even," he assured her. It only made her cry harder.

Without letting go, she turned to look at Theo. He was staring at all the kids, craning his neck back and forth like he was trying to count them. It must have been weird, seeing all the shadows in your house become flesh. But probably no weirder than it had been being a shadow himself. On impulse, she wrapped him in a hug too. Just quickly and tightly enough that he blinked at her with reddening cheeks.

"Good to see you, too, Micah. I thought I was going to be a ghost in my own house forever."

"I'd never let that happen." She hadn't quite been as sure at the time, but what was a little reassurance after a much-needed win? "Besides, what are new friends for?"

He smiled, but it faded just as quickly as he looked over her shoulder. She turned. Jenn was still behind her. She was looking at Poppop, tense and silent. Micah half expected the house to shake with the force of whatever Jenn was feeling until she remembered that she was the one connected to it now.

The thought startled her. She tried to make herself neutral just in case Finch House decided to mimic how she felt.

"Um." She didn't need to give introductions, obviously, but she felt like she should say *something*.

"I'm so sorry, Jenn," Poppop said before she could. "I . . . you . . ."

To Micah's surprise, his face fell. She had seen Poppop cry before, but she had never seen him like this, with his face so scrunched up and his eyes full of tears. He looked sad, yes, but he also looked so angry with himself that Micah's heart hurt.

His expression didn't change as he took a deep breath and lowered himself to his knees until he and Jenn were face-to-face.

"You should know that I've thought about you every single day, Jenn. On my worst days and on the best days of my life. Not once did I forget about you. Or what I did to you. I wish I could tell you that I came back, that I tried to look for you, but . . ." He shook his head. "Even if it wasn't allowed, I should've tried. I *could've* tried so much harder than I did."

He reached for her hand but caught himself and stopped. His throat bobbed as he swallowed. "I know it's too little, too late, but I shouldn't have left you. Not for a second." He chuckled softly, a sadder sound than a laugh was meant to be. "Especially not with all the times you had the chance to leave me growing up and didn't.

"I'm sorry, Jenn. I couldn't tell you enough how sorry I am and have been all these years."

Jenn stared at her little brother, years and years older than she was now. Her eyes were teary, but her expression was angry. If she and Finch House were still connected, Micah had no doubt the walls would be shaking as much as her hands were. And she understood it now, too. Just how deep her great-aunt's anger went. The image of Poppop running away wasn't one she'd forget anytime soon.

"You're an idiot," Jenn said finally. She punched Poppop once in the arm and then again and again until she was crying, and then they were hugging, her face buried into his shoulder as she cried.

"I was so scared," she whispered. "I was so alone."

"I'm sorry," Poppop said. Over and over. "I'm sorry."

Micah looked away to give them privacy and felt Theo at her side. They didn't talk. They only watched the other people—ghosts—move from group to group and inch closer and closer to the open door.

"So, what did you do?" he asked finally.

Micah kept her eyes on the door. They widened when a familiar-looking teenager with feathered hair and wide-legged jeans took a careful step toward the door, closer than any of the others. But Callie didn't move any closer. Not yet.

"What do you mean, what did I do?"

"To save us. I don't think Finch House just changed its mind because you asked nicely."

"It kind of did."

Theo looked at her. It was still such a relief to see him as himself again, wary and shy and determined. And her secret was hot enough on her tongue that it would burn her if she didn't tell someone else.

"I made a deal," she said as simply as she could.

"*What?*"

Heads whipped toward them, and Micah quickly shushed him.

"*What?*" he said again, a whisper that was no less full of outrage or surprise. "What kind of deal? Don't you watch movies? Don't you know you shouldn't make deals with houses or ghosts or whoever you did it with?"

His eyes widened. "Are you going to be stuck in my house now? Because I have no idea how I would explain that to my parents and Renee. Or your mom!"

Quietly and as quickly as she could, she told Theo everything. Saying it aloud to someone else, it still sounded like the best choice. She couldn't find any flaws or remember any hidden loopholes during her retelling.

Poppop and Theo were free. Jenn hadn't suddenly disappeared. She didn't even think she was tied to the house for six months out of the year like some sort of modern Persephone, her least favorite Greek goddess.

When Theo only blinked at her, she huffed. "Well? Are you going to say something?"

"Does this mean my house won't be haunted anymore?"

She nodded.

"And that you *can* actually leave?"

She nodded again.

"Then I think . . . I think it sounds okay. Maybe. You just have to keep your eyes open for the bad parts."

That wasn't reassuring. She told him as much.

He shrugged. "I just mean everything has bad parts, even the really good things."

Micah rolled her eyes. "Remind me to ask you what you think about a glass of water."

Before either of them could say anything else, there

was a burst of light and a rush of sound that left Micah's ears ringing and her eyes watering. She squinted through it just enough to watch Callie step through the door into . . . somewhere.

All of Finch House was silent.

Watchful.

Waiting.

"Do you know where she went?" Theo whispered in her ear. Micah shook her head.

However Finch House had created the door, wherever it had pulled it from, it had no connection to what was beyond it. It was, she assumed, the next step in letting everyone go.

After a moment, everyone released their collective breath. People went back to talking . . . and then they all started to get in line. Micah and Theo watched them step through the door one by one for a while before she turned back to Poppop and Jenn. They weren't hugging anymore. They weren't even talking. Jenn's eyes were fixed firmly on the door again, and Poppop's were on her.

"It's okay to be scared, Jenn," he said softly.

"*I* told *you* that," she grumbled. "And I'm not scared. I lived here forever, didn't I?" She took half a step forward and stopped, looking around. She smiled faintly when her eyes met Micah's.

"I guess I'm a little scared," she admitted. "Leaving . . . I never really thought it was something I'd get to do."

Not for the first time, Micah thought about how scared and lost she'd been in the hallway. And how similar those feelings were to Jenn's, scared and lost in the basement. She thought of the different deals Finch House had made with each of them and how easily she could have ended up like her: an angry, lonely girl who stole people for company. A ghost willing to trap someone else if it meant having the slightest bit of responsibility taken off her shoulders.

"I can walk with you," Micah offered. "As far as the door."

The line had gone quickly. There had been dozens of people standing and waiting for their turn at whatever was beyond Finch House, but now there was only Jenn.

Like it had been in the beginning.

Jenn nodded, and Micah stepped forward to take her hand. It was strangely solid in hers. Both their hands shook with the force of Jenn's nerves.

Micah took a step forward, and Jenn followed half a second later. Before they could take the next, Jenn paused again and turned to look at Poppop.

"I'm glad you got to live your life, Elijah."

There was no "I forgive you," but it sounded like forgiveness to Micah.

With a deep breath and a tighter grip on Micah's hand, Jenn stepped forward again. Micah let her take the lead until they were both standing in front of the door.

This close, she could feel cool air, but that was all. There was no sound and no smell. She took a deep breath but tasted nothing on her tongue. The lack of anything made her nervous. There was nothing to hint at what might be on the other side.

She felt her own grip tighten. Jenn's did the same in response.

"Are you sure about this?" she blurted out. "It's just that . . ."

It's just that who knew what came next? Being stuck in Finch House wasn't the best thing, sure, but what if she walked through the door and ended up somewhere even worse?

"Maybe you should take a day. Think about it some more."

Jenn laughed. "I've thought about this for longer than you can imagine. I'm ready to leave Finch House."

She took a deep breath. "No matter what comes next."

Micah bit her lip and nodded. She couldn't be nervous for other people. Her mom had told her that a million times. Everyone's choices were their own just like hers were her own. She couldn't worry about the world, no matter how often her brain told her that she should at least try.

But this wasn't the world. This was her aunt. They didn't know each other at all, really, and Jenn had been willing to risk Micah's freedom just for a taste of her own.

But they both loved Poppop.

And they were the only people that they knew of who'd made deals with Finch House.

They were connected, the two of them.

By blood and by a house.

"I guess I should say sorry," Jenn said, meeting Micah's gaze almost nervously.

"You don't have to just because I'm helping you leave."

Her great-aunt shook her head. "I want to. It's just . . . sorry feels pretty small for all the things I did." She glanced around the room, at the empty space where the kids she'd trapped in Finch House had been standing until recently. "And all the people I did them to. I didn't really mean to . . ."

She trailed off. When she stayed quiet, Micah pulled Jenn into a hug.

She felt a rush of emotion—anger and sadness and relief all at once. She knew that everything could have gone very differently, very wrong. But it hadn't. That was what was important. Besides, she'd gotten a small glimpse into why Jenn had made the decisions she did. She wasn't entirely sure she would have made different ones if their roles were reversed.

"I can't forgive you for everyone else," she said, "and I'm not sure I forgive you for myself, either. But I'm glad we met."

Jenn was quiet, but her hug felt a little tighter.

"Be careful," she said when the hug ended, already facing the door again. "And take care of Elijah for me. I don't want to see him again for a long time, you know?"

Before Micah could make any new promises, Jenn squeezed her hand a final time. Then she was gone, through the door with only the slightest breeze left in her wake. Micah watched the door swing shut, the faint glow around it fading until it was just plain wood.

On her wrist again, Nana's bracelet burned with the

same warmth Micah felt in her chest. She looked down. A new charm had been added. A small version of the key she'd used to unlock the turret room, the tiny finch on the end staring up at her in silence. She turned the key over in her hand, watching it twirl and glow gold from the overhead lights.

It wasn't much quieter in the house without the ghosts.

It wasn't much different at all.

Except that if she shut her eyes, she saw the shadow-and-sunlight woman finishing up a painting of the door with an eye for a peephole.

When it opened, it looked directly at her.

"Well done," said Finch House.

chapter eighteen

As nervous as Micah had been about the move, she found that she was too busy on the day itself to do much worrying. The movers Mom had hired, with their baseball caps and silent determination, went in and out of the house, carrying things up and down the stairs. The bed went into her bedroom, the couches and the bookshelf and the coffee table went in the living room.

When she wasn't helping, Micah watched. She hadn't realized just how much *stuff* they had.

She set the latest box down and hopped onto her bare mattress. From there she could see out her window into the backyard. It was tiny, but it had a small garden and a neighbor's tree brushed the top of their fence, both currently covered in snow. She tried to picture herself out there in the spring, reading or watching the clouds. She could almost do it.

She looked around her box-filled room. It was bigger than her room at Poppop's had been, with a window nook just big enough for the purple beanbag chair she'd gotten. Someone had left flower stickers on the inside of the closet door, and in certain spots glitter sparkled in the carpet, but she liked those things about her new room, those strange little touches. They felt like proof that someone had been happy there before her and that she could be happy there too.

There was a knock at the door. She turned in time to see Theo peeking his head in. "Your mom's looking for you, Micah." He smiled apologetically. "She wants to know if you think the rest of us are going to bring all your stuff up for you."

She hopped off her bed with a sigh. "I don't see why you wanted to help us move. I told you my mom gets cranky when she's stressed."

She followed him back to the front of the house. Her mom was talking to one of the movers, gesturing toward the truck with both hands. Her hair had been up in a bun on the ride there, but half her curls were in her face and brushing her shoulders now.

"I thought you could use the help. And it was better than freezing outside."

Micah hadn't been back inside Finch House in a week, but she knew Theo still spent most of his time outside. She found him in the front yard with Paprika whenever she rode her bike by to ask if he wanted to ride with her.

That first day, she'd half expected Finch House to swallow her up the second she got close, or to talk to her again, but neither happened. Almost nothing had happened, in fact, since the day she'd made the deal. She was tempted to consider the whole thing a dream if her mom wasn't still "holding on to her phone for a while" until she learned to actually answer when she called.

And if Poppop didn't give her a look every now and then like he was trying to figure her out. They still hadn't talked about what had happened in Finch House. She wasn't sure they were ever going to, even though she had found herself standing outside his bedroom door in the middle of the night a few times, just on the edge of knocking.

She never knocked.

The dreams she had now weren't scary. She could deal with them on her own.

"You could go inside now," she said finally, stacking two light boxes one on top of the other. She could barely

184

see him over all the cardboard. "All the shadows are gone, right?"

She didn't have to ask; she knew they were. She knew a lot more about Finch House now than she ever had before, even when she wasn't thinking about it, even when she wasn't anywhere nearby. Just at that moment she knew that someone had turned the water on in one of the upstairs bathrooms and that someone else was in the kitchen.

"Yeah," Theo agreed. He tossed an oversize tote bag over his shoulder and stumbled at the weight. "I just remember, is all."

She nodded. Some things were hard to forget.

By the time they took a break for lunch, the winter sun was close to setting, and all Micah wanted to do was lie on the floor until everything stopped hurting. So, she did, surrounded by boxes and furniture instructions and packing tape. She opened her eyes with a smile when she felt someone standing over her and sat up, patting the spot next to her. Carefully, Poppop sat.

At her mom's insistence, he'd mostly told the movers where to put things. He was too old, she'd said, to lift heavy things. She liked his bones as unbroken and unbruised as possible. Looking at him, Micah agreed. He looked different than he had just a week ago, when moving was her biggest worry and Finch House was still a mystery. Maybe it was just that she couldn't shake how gray and dead-eyed he'd been in the basement. Or maybe it was because of the new white hair in his mustache or the dip between his eyebrows. Whatever it was, Micah understood that he had lived a long life. And she understood that he might not have as much of it left as she did.

The thought came with tears. She shoved both to the side. He was there now, in front of her, next to her, and that was what mattered. She couldn't live her life in fast-forward all the time, Dr. Roberts had said at their first meeting a few days ago, or she'd miss all the best parts.

"All worn out, Turtle?" Poppop asked. He was wearing her favorite smile, the one that looked like he could laugh at any second.

She groaned. "I've never been so tired in my whole life. I never want to move again."

He laughed. "Moving will do that. Halfway there, though."

She nodded, and they sat in silence. Micah tried to keep an ear out for any noises the new house was making, but all she could hear was the game Theo was playing on his phone and the rustling sounds of unpacking her mom was making in the kitchen.

"I've got something for you," Poppop said finally. "I'd planned to wait, but, well, it's probably easiest if I give it to you now, before I head home."

He held out his hands. In them was a photo album. Not the same one she'd snuck out of his room but a similar one. She took it eagerly.

On the first page was a picture of him and Aunt Jenn. He was younger than he'd been in the Finch House memory and smiling widely at her while she stared straight at the camera, her own smile barely visible. She looked exactly the same and completely different. She looked like a kid.

They went through the album together between bites of sandwiches and sips of water. Poppop and Aunt Jenn and their family. Road trips and holidays and chicken chasing. And he had a story to go along with all of the photos, some that made him laugh and others that made him go quiet.

When they'd flipped to the very last page, Micah looked at him. "How come you've never shown me these before? Or Mom?"

He stared down at the album. The last picture was of him leaning far out over the edge of a fence, waving at something out of frame.

"I felt guilty," he said after a long moment. "And ashamed. I didn't think I deserved to look at these anymore."

For a moment, Micah thought he might bring up Finch House and everything that had happened inside it. But he didn't. Instead, he shut the front cover and placed the photo album in her lap.

"But they're your family too, and they deserve to be remembered. Besides, I figured you and your mom ought to have some family with you out here at your new place."

Micah pulled Poppop into a hug, the album wedged between them.

The new house wouldn't be the same, of course. It couldn't be without Poppop right down the hall. But she was starting to realize that change didn't have to mean bad. Even when it was scary. Even when it meant missing someone. Mostly, change just meant going forward.

She hugged Poppop a little tighter. He wasn't leaving yet. They still had so much to bring inside. But she didn't know how else to thank him—not just for the photo album and the stories, but for being her grand-father.

"All right," he said, smiling, when they pulled apart. "Eat up. I think your mom's running out of things to unpack in that kitchen, and she's going to put you two back to work."

Micah wasn't sure if it was just because they were trying to beat the quickly setting sun or because they knew the house a little better, but the second half of moving day went quicker. They became a machine, her, her mom, and Theo, with Poppop supervising. Boxes were moved quickly from the car into the house and into their rightful rooms.

She was walking backward into the house and shar-ing the weight of a bin with Theo when she saw him. A man who looked a little less real than everything else around him.

At first Micah thought it was Finch House. She could *feel* Finch House like something she carried in her pocket and brushed her hands against sometimes. It was a tiny weight inside her, a thought whenever her mind wan-dered or right before she went to bed. She knew she could talk to it if she wanted, even from far away, and that it would answer, but she hadn't tried yet. She preferred not to think too much about it in the hope that it didn't think too much about her, either.

But even though he had the same wispiness of shadows clinging to him, she couldn't feel this man. There was no connection to him like there was between her and Finch House. Which relieved her. And then, of course, made her curious.

She hadn't realized she'd been staring until Theo jostled the bin they were both holding, and she tightened her grip before it could land on her foot.

"Are you okay?" he asked. "You've been standing there staring for a whole minute without saying anything."

Had it been that long? It had felt like just a second, just a glance. She looked over his shoulder again. The man was still there, more shadow than sunlight. She couldn't tell if he was looking her way or not, but she shivered anyway.

"Do you see that guy?" she asked.

Theo looked over his shoulder. "What guy?"

"He looks like Finch House."

Theo frowned. Dark hair fell into his face. He tried to shake it free without his hands and failed. "Like a ghost?"

She shook her head. She'd seen ghosts. She'd seen plenty of them now. But Finch House wasn't like that. It was its own thing—shadowy but solid, a spirit of something that wasn't a person.

Except maybe it wasn't its own thing.

Maybe there were other shadow-and-sunlight people out there. Other keepers for things besides houses.

"I don't know how to explain it," she said finally, stepping backward into the house. "But there's definitely a guy over there."

By the time they put the bin down and went back outside, the man was gone, and there was too much to do for Micah to keep thinking about him.

"Okay," Micah said, sitting in the finally empty bed of Poppop's truck. So high up from the ground, it was easy to swing her legs while she tried to think of her next steps. "I'll be back at Poppop's two weekends from now," she told Theo. "We're having a movie marathon on Friday, but we can hang out on Saturday."

She'd decided to leave the chest at Poppop's house. She and Poppop had made a promise to each other. A new one. They'd work their way through the chest and all the movies in it—some were Micah's favorites, others she'd never heard of—a weekend at a time. It made her feel better, knowing that they'd still have some weekends together. And keeping some of her things there made it feel like it was still her home.

"You can meet my friends, Maggie and Dante," Micah said. "I think they'll be back from vacation by then. Maybe even Elisa."

Theo didn't suggest hanging out at his house, and neither did she. As empty as Finch House was now, except for the people who lived in it, she couldn't see herself in there anytime soon.

"Micah?" her mom called her. "C'mon, it's getting late. Poppop and Theo have to head out."

Taking a deep breath, she followed her mom's voice and leaned into her side when she found her, watching Theo climb into her usual seat next to Poppop. Her mom wrapped an arm around her and gave her a quick squeeze.

"Excited to have our own house?"

She was worried. And she was curious. And she really hoped they were the only people living in it.

But, yeah, she was excited, too.

She smiled. "Definitely."

Her mom pressed a kiss to the top of her head and

turned to go inside once Poppop's truck had faded from sight. Micah started to follow her and paused. Something in the corner of her eye moved. Quick enough to be a cat or a squirrel. She narrowed her eyes to get a better look and walked down the driveway. Their house was at the end of a street surrounded by a ton of trees.

Maybe it was a deer.

But anxiety twisted her stomach into knots. Her heart pounded in her chest, and the noise echoed in her ears.

It definitely wasn't a deer, she knew.

The tiny door in her head that she kept firmly shut, the one marked FINCH HOUSE, slowly creaked open.

Micah didn't scream when the mostly shadow man appeared a few feet in front of her.

Not when he met her gaze, his eyes the bright green of summertime grass.

Not when he smiled.

Not even when he spoke and his voice was both in the world and in her head.

"Well, isn't this a surprise. Welcome home."

Acknowledgments

This book wouldn't exist without the help and love of so many people, first and foremost my family. Everyone who knows me knows that I am a Family Oriented Sim and my love for every person in my family is beyond words. Thank you all for fostering my creativity, answering my random "what if" questions, listening to all my rants, and just being yourselves. You are all so much weirder than any characters I could ever write and I love you for it.

Thank you to my amazing agent, Patrice Caldwell, for your support and championing of my work. I used to dream about working with you and I still can't believe I get to, honestly! Thank you to Trinica Sampson for your kindness, efficiency, and ability to somehow make emails not the worst thing ever, and to everyone at New Leaf, including but not limited to Veronica Grijalva, Pouya Shahbazian, and Katherine Curtis.

An enormous, gigantic thank-you to Kate Prosswimmer, editor extraordinaire. This book wouldn't be anywhere near as good without you and your comments/ suggestions/praise. From our first phone call, I knew I wanted to work with you. Thank you for taking a chance on me and Micah. Thank you to everyone at McElderry Books, known and unknown to me, including Justin Chanda, Karen Wojtyla, Nicole Florica, Anum Shafqat, and Bridget Madsen.

Thank you to Alessia Trunfio for this absolutely gorgeous cover! You brought Micah and Theo and Finch House to life with your amazing art and I will never be over it. Thanks, too, to Greg Stadynk for designing such a wonderful cover.

A special, unending thank-you to my friends, both in real life and on Discord (a different kind of real life): Molly, Cynthia, Alex, Julie, Lana, Sabrina, Natalie, Anna, and Bianca. You've all listened to me rant, whine, stress, and fangirl with the patience and enthusiasm of saints. I'm grateful for your friendship, media recs, and random Discord brainstorming.

Thank you also to my friends and former bookseller coworkers—Katherine, McKenna, both Brittanys, and Sean—for dealing with closing-shift me, hyping my writing up, and creating our delightful virtual pandemic book club. Thank you too to my Emerson friends—

Nihal, Madeline, Christina, Prerna, and Dave—who haven't read this book (yet) but supported me through another one so much that the support spilled over into this one, too.

Thanks to Pepper, the real life Paprika and the best (furry) family member. You can't read and didn't actually help me do anything, but you've kept me company plenty of times over the past sixteen years.

These acknowledgments wouldn't be complete without me shouting out my mom. Hi, Mom! Thank you for so easily accepting writing as my love language and for all those lunch box notes; you'll never know how much they meant to me. And for your constant reiteration of "You write, don't you? Then you're a writer." That one's helped me work my way through so much self-doubt.

Perhaps the biggest thank-you is to my poppop. This book began with you and my memories of us networking together. Thank you for that cross—not an *x*!—and for the love you've filled this family with and for the house where we all gather. I'm *so* glad it's not haunted. Even if I'm kind of doubtful about the basement.

And, finally, to the readers, especially if you've made it this far. Thank you so much for walking down those stairs with Micah.